HER
Thankful
Heart

VALERIE COMER

GreenWords Media

Give thanks to the LORD,
for he is good,
For his steadfast love endures forever.
Psalm 136:1 ESV

Free story?

Excited to read an entire romance series with characters in their 50s? I'm excited to write it! I'd love to offer you a free ebook novella to introduce the Christmas at Maranatha Inn series. The story is called *Her Waiting Heart*. Find out more and grab your copy at:

https://valeriecomer.com/waiting

CHAPTER
One

Pamela Whorley pulled open the door to the small-town diner, stepped inside, blinked, and did a double take.

Oh. My. Goodness.

The place looked like the entire Golden Girls sitcom from the 1980s had exploded inside its walls. Nice play on words for the Golden Grill, or it would have been if it wasn't so tacky.

Pam's fingers itched to rip posters and memorabilia off the walls and shelves. Anything to rid the atmosphere of kaleidoscopic chaos. She could scarcely breathe.

She may have promised Julia she'd stay at nearby Maranatha Inn through the end of the year and get the restaurant up and running, but if this was a sign of the townspeople's expectations, they wouldn't appreciate the upscale dining Pam had planned. Hopefully, marketing would bring in the type of clientele who would welcome what her skills had to offer. A different group than frequented here, for certain.

"Welcome to the Golden Grill." A middle-aged woman all but bounced beside the hostess desk. "Table for one?"

Always a table for one. Ever since Mark — Pam chopped off the memory. It had been years. She should be used to it by now.

She inhaled. Exhaled. Focused on the woman, who appeared about her own age. "Yes, please."

"Window or wall?"

Pam glanced around. She was early for the lunch rush, if this place even had one. A young family sat around a table at the other end. A group of cowboys laughed and drank coffee in the corner booth. A gray-haired man and two tweens sat at a high-top.

"Window, please." Surely a view of the park across the street would feel less claustrophobic than having the four starlets staring down at her, larger than life. Plus, she'd be farther from the other diners.

"Right this way. I'm Estelle. I don't think I've seen you in here before."

Estelle. No doubt, the woman thought it was clever sharing a name with one of the sitcom's actors.

Pam managed a stiff smile. She'd only been to Jewel Lake once before, for Julia's husband's funeral. She slid onto the padded bench the hostess indicated. "May I have a coffee, please? And a menu?"

Estelle's smile faltered slightly. "Of course. I'll be right back." She wove past the other tables on her way to the kitchen. "Granger, honey, can I get you or the kids anything else?"

"Ice cream?" the boy wheedled, glancing at the man hopefully. He looked to be about nine, his sister maybe two years older.

Pam gulped and turned to look outside. Even a dozen years later, kids this age got to her. Would the hole in her heart ever heal?

Ground yourself. Five things you see.

That was easy with a window view. Trees with golden leaves, glowing in the October sun. A blue, blue sky. Two women chatting on a park bench. A glimpse of the lake beyond the park. A—

"Here you go, ma'am." Estelle set the coffee and a menu in front of her. "I didn't catch your name."

Because Pam hadn't given it. Because she didn't make instant friends. "Thank you."

"Our lunch special today is a Reuben sandwich with fries and your choice of a cup of soup or a side salad."

Just like that, Pam's memories insisted on resurfacing. Her daughter had been obsessed with Reubens, comparing them from the various restaurants they'd visited. How long had it been since Pam had opted for one? Forever.

She slid the menu to the edge. "I'll try the special." *For you, Courtney, because that girl over there reminds me of you.*

"The soup of the day is chicken noodle."

The soup was likely out of a can. Pam managed not to flinch. "Sounds good. Thank you."

"It will just be a few minutes, Ms..." Estelle lingered, obviously hopeful.

Pam smiled at her then turned back to the window. Where was she? Right. Five audible things.

"Thank you, Gramps!"

"Mom would never let us have ice cream so close to lunch."

"I'm not your mother."

Pam dragged her focus away from the threesome. She could hear the hiss of the grill in the kitchen. Laughter from one of the cowboys. Five sounds, if she counted each voice separately.

Five smells. That was harder. Could a person actually smell the decor? The atmosphere? It seemed like she could. She inhaled the aroma of coffee. Mark had liked his with sugar and cream.

Pam forced herself back to the diner. She could usually block the memories better than this. Why the struggle here, today? Wasn't the whole purpose of moving across the country to get away from the past and make a new start where no one knew her?

She scoffed lightly under her breath. Okay, that was a lie. Julia had known her in college, and she hadn't invited only Pam to celebrate her new venture opening the Maranatha Inn, but their entire college friend-group from way back when.

It should have been okay. None of those women had known Mark well. They'd all gotten together occasionally over the years, but Pam's college friends hadn't been woven into her daily life.

They didn't know how close to the rocks Pam and Mark's marriage had been. They didn't know anything other than the horrific crash that had taken Mark and both kids in the blink of an eye, leaving Pam reeling.

Her friends had gathered round for the funeral, but Pam had been strong. She hadn't leaned on them. Hadn't dumped the whole sordid tale on them. Only Christina had guarded her. The others had probed and begged Pam to cry and let it all out. Chris told them to back off and let Pam grieve her own way.

Too bad her own way hadn't worked. Oh, she'd been functioning. She'd poured herself into her catering business then sold it to take on a job as chef in a Michelin-starred restaurant. But Julia insisted there was more to life than work, and here Pam was, thousands of miles from South Carolina, gripping a coffee cup with nearly enough force to crush it.

Five things you can touch.

The mug wasn't run-of-the-mill. She folded her hands around the hand-thrown pottery. Felt the warmth. Felt the pressure of her fingertips.

"Ma'am?"

Pam looked up as Estelle set down a plate with a fragrant golden sandwich with hand-cut French fries and a bowl of chicken noodle soup. Wow. Pam had vastly underestimated this establishment. That delectable aroma had definitely not come from a supermarket shelf.

"This smells delicious. My name is Pam." Relieving the woman's curiosity seemed the least she could do considering the mouthwatering feast in front of her. "I'm in town for an extended visit." Three months. Probably not a minute longer.

"I'm so pleased to meet you, Pam. I hope we'll be good friends."

Pam already had five of those at Maranatha Inn just outside town. How many did a woman need? Especially a woman who was a widow... and it had never seemed fair that there was a word for a husbandless wife but not a word for a childless mother.

Was there a word for unfriendly friend? Because Pam was going to have to do better if she truly wanted a fresh start. She managed a smile at Estelle and opened her mouth to respond to the woman's overture.

A crash came from the high-top in the middle, and Estelle whirled around. A bowl lay shattered on the floor in a puddle of melting ice cream.

"I'm sorry, Gramps! I didn't mean to." The boy's lips trembled.

"You're so clumsy." The self-righteous older sister glanced at her grandfather as though for approval. "You never pay attention."

"I'm not clumsy! It was an accident."

"It's okay, Oliver." The older man grabbed a handful of napkins from the dispenser and lowered himself to the floor.

If Pam didn't miss her guess, the man — Granger? — had a sore knee. His movement seemed stilted, awkward.

"Here, let me." Estelle bustled to the kitchen and returned with cleaning supplies. She dropped to the floor and tackled the multi-colored puddle.

"I'm sorry, Estelle." The man hoisted himself upright, grimacing as he did so.

Yep. Either he was simply ancient enough to have creaky joints as a rite of passage — way older than Pam's 54 — or he'd suffered an injury somewhere along the line.

"I'm sorry, too," the boy mumbled, cringing back into his chair as his sister glowered at him.

"It's okay, little man." Estelle smiled up at the kid.

She had way more patience than Pam would have. There'd been a reason Pam preferred cooking to waiting tables, and not because serving was beneath her. There were too many unpredictable people. Too many uncontrollable messes.

Granger met her gaze across the room. He offered a small smile with a shake of his head.

Pam read that as, "Kids. What can you do?"

Well, one could discipline them. Being a grandparent didn't mean the kids should run roughshod all over a person. She'd made sure both her parents and Mark's had understood that.

Fat lot of good it had done.

Granger Durand tore his gaze from the pretty woman over by the window. He wasn't in Jewel Lake to start something with anyone and, from the little he'd overheard, she was here temporarily, anyway.

He shook his head again. Not that he was sure how long he'd be around, himself. Melissa guarded herself against him, and he could hardly blame her. What kind of man chose the military over his own daughter? Over his wife? Denise had known what being a military spouse would be like. She'd chosen Granger anyway... then promptly unchosen him in favor of a man who offered her more stability and more money. Denise had also unchosen Granger as the father of his child... and he'd allowed her.

It was too late to undo those years.

But not too late to make amends, if Melissa would let him. Not too late to know his grandkids... if Melissa would let him.

She wasn't super excited about having him around, but as a recent divorcée herself, she could use her old dad's help here and there, whether she wanted to admit it or not.

Granger would give her until the New Year. He wouldn't be able to justify his current lodgings indefinitely, so he'd have to figure out something else by then. Somehow, he'd stay in western Montana and keep in contact with Sidney and Oliver.

It wasn't like there was anyplace else to call home. A career in the military did that to a man... at least, if he let it consume him.

And Granger had. He'd welcomed it, in fact, after Denise had moved on.

He shifted restlessly on the chair and massaged his kneecap. There was nothing for him anywhere but here. He'd found a church home at Creekside Fellowship. Melissa had been allowing the kids to attend with him, though Sidney resisted.

Hope existed in Jewel Lake, even if it seemed dim and insubstantial at times.

Over by the window, the uptight woman began carving her sandwich with a knife and fork.

Granger blinked.

"Why doesn't she just pick it up?" Oliver's question rang too loud.

The woman shot a glare in their direction.

She'd looked pretty before. Not stunning, but nice in a no-nonsense kind of way. Trim and petite. Designer slacks and sweater top. Short hair that managed to remain feminine.

Glowering did not improve her features.

But then, Oliver had not been making the best first impression.

Granger scoffed at himself. She was temporary, and there wouldn't likely be a chance for a second impression. Not that it mattered. He wasn't interested. Wasn't looking.

Although, why not? He knew a dozen reasons why not with the woman by the window, but in general? He was only 59, and he'd been alone a long time. He might have 20 or 30 years ahead of him yet — possibly even more — and was companionship during his remaining years too much to hope for?

He hadn't truly thought about marriage since Denise's Dear John letter had arrived on base. Their relationship had been shaky from the start. Before it, even. He'd almost been relieved when she'd called him off. Told him Grant would be their unborn child's father, and it would be less confusing for the baby if Granger kept right on staying out of his or her life.

But this woman wasn't Denise. "I'm sorry, ma'am. The boy needs to learn respect."

The woman's eyebrows tipped up in acknowledgment. She lifted her spoon.

"They make great soup here, don't they? All from scratch."

The spoon poised halfway to her mouth. She looked at him again. Probably wondering why he was making small talk.

Uh… good question. Granger held up his hand to acknowledge his strangeness and turned back to the kids. "Ready to go? We can hang out in the park for a few minutes if you like."

Sidney sniffed her disapproval. Practicing to be a teenager, that girl.

But Oliver's face brightened. "Can we?"

"Sure. Your mother isn't expecting us back for another half hour."

"Ollie, you're such a *child*," Sidney muttered, rolling her eyes.

Because he was one. Should Granger call his granddaughter out? Man, he didn't know how to relate to these kids. He'd never had much to do with preteens before, and he was learning as he went. Hopefully, any mistakes he made wouldn't be too devastating long term. His well-intentioned errors had to be better than continued absence.

He tugged his wallet out of his hip pocket as he rose. Oliver and Sidney ejected off of their tall chairs and dashed toward the exit, pushing and shoving.

"Kids!" he bellowed.

Too late. With a well-timed hip check, Sidney sent Oliver stumbling into the woman's elbow. Her spoon flew out of her hand and clattered against the window, leaving a spatter of noodles and shredded chicken across the table.

She surged to her feet, face suffused with anger.

Granger could hardly blame her. His grandchildren acted like little savages. Even now, they careened out the door without seeming to notice the mayhem they'd caused. They certainly hadn't apologized.

Leaving Granger to do so on their behalf. "I'm so sorry. I don't know what got into them, but their behavior is inexcusable."

"Someone needs to teach those hooligans some manners." Her blue eyes spat daggers.

"You're absolutely right." *A gentle answer turns away wrath, but a harsh word stirs up anger.* How many times had that proverb come to mind at exactly the right instant? "I truly hope your day improves from here." He hesitated, but couldn't think of anything to add. He could wipe up the soup, but it didn't look like she'd welcome his further interference. Besides, Estelle scurried their direction.

So Granger did the only thing he could think of. He quietly paid for her lunch along with his and the kids' snack before following them out the door.

CHAPTER
Two

P am stared at the edifice in front of her. Julia had sent photos of the Maranatha Inn under construction as well as numerous shots of the finished building to their group chat, but somehow, Pam still hadn't expected something so big. So grand.

The Coxes must have had more money than Pam had ever suspected. Sad that George hadn't lived to see his life's dream completed. He had died of a massive heart attack shortly after they'd purchased the land, but ground for the inn had not yet broken when Pam had come for his funeral.

The door slid open, and Julia flew down the steps toward her, so Pam exited her car and readied herself for the inevitable crushing embrace.

"I can't believe you're here!" Julia squealed. "How was your trip? Are you hungry? What do you think of all this?" She waved toward the massive white building with its angles, porches, bows, and turrets.

Pam couldn't help laughing as she squeezed back. "I'm good. It was a long drive, but I got to see a lot of the country at a beautiful time of year. Your inn looks amazing, and I stopped for an early lunch in Jewel Lake." Had she covered all the bases?

"You had lunch in town? Where, the Golden Grill? Isn't that place simply darling?"

Pam opened her mouth and closed it again. Best to consider her words carefully. "The food was excellent."

"Yes, Leo is a great chef. Not in your class, of course."

Running a small-town diner had never been one of Pam's aspirations. With an arm wrapped around her friend, she turned toward the inn. "Show me everything!"

"Isn't it magnificent?" Julia swiped at her eyes. "I wish George…"

Pam squeezed. "I'm sorry."

"I know you understand, what with Mark's passing and all."

At least Julia hadn't lost her entire family in one go. Which didn't mean her pain wasn't real. It was certainly more recent.

"It seems so strange." Julia sounded wistful. "We were all such good friends in college, and now here we all are, solo again." She managed to brighten her tone. "Chris, as you know, is already onsite. Audrey and Wendy are on their way, and Laura… well, I hope she actually comes."

"I haven't seen Wendy in years. We were so close in college, but then she and Dave moved to Oregon."

They'd had six kids before Dave cheated on her, dumped her, and married someone else 20 years younger. If Pam had a chance to kick the cheater where it hurt, she'd definitely wear her pointiest shoes. She hadn't played soccer in years, but she'd bet her life that she could still place her toes exactly where she wanted them.

"It will be like old home week." Julia hugged Pam again. "Except longer. I'm so excited to have our gang all together again at last."

"Me, too." They'd talked about this dream on and off for years, but Pam had never expected it to happen. Never expected to move all the way to western Montana herself. Temporarily, she amended in her thoughts. This wasn't a *move* move. Just a few months to help Julia get things off the ground until she found the perfect chef. Never know, though. It wasn't like there was any reason to return to South Carolina. Even her parents were gone.

But Julia was tugging her toward the front door under a portico. A huge sign proclaiming, "Welcome to Maranatha Inn," hung above it.

Maranatha. The Lord is coming.

It seemed a strange name for a boutique hotel, but Julia loved the nod to the advent season. She was Christmas crazy. Always had been. Her room in college had been so packed with a tree and angel ornaments and lights and... it had short-circuited Pam's brain as well as the dorm's electrical system.

And now here she was, willingly putting herself into the orbit of Julia's effervescent Christmas spirit. Surely her friend had learned that less was more sometime in the past 30 years? Remembering college, though, Pam could only be surprised that it was October first and there were no decorations in sight.

That thought vanished with a poof the moment she stepped into the lobby. A giant fake tree filled the space between the windows across the space.

She turned to her friend, eyebrows raised. "Already?"

Julia giggled. "You know me. It's never too early to prepare for Christ's arrival."

Pam could beg to differ with that, but she'd save her breath. "I'm trying to see the actual inn. You know, the parts that aren't covered with twinkle lights."

"I kept the kitchen simple. Wanna see?"

"Do birds live to fly? Point the way." What did simple mean, anyway?

Julia waved a hand. "So, the lobby is here on the left. We've been lighting a fire in the evenings. The leather love seats are super comfy. The live-edge tables were made by a local artisan. Same with the stained-glass hangings in the windows."

"Very nice. You mentioned a kitchen?"

"The dining room is on the right. We'll require reservations for dinner, so you'll always know the number you'll be feeding."

The round-ended room was filled with small circular tables layered with white linen cloths. Christmas plaid napkins sat at every place along with crystal goblets and white China. Pam followed Julia across the space to the state-of-the-art kitchen. After one quick look around, she turned and embraced her friend. "I love you."

Julia snickered. "I love you, too. I take it this meets with your approval?"

"Great layout. Great appliances."

"All of which you helped pick out."

"Right, but until you actually see the finished space, you're never sure."

"Good point. That's how I feel about all of this."

"When do you need me to start cooking?"

"Wednesday night? We'll be open for dinners Wednesday through Sunday. We do have a breakfast chef seven days a week, but that's only for staff and guests. We only have three of those right now, but we'll have our grand opening at Thanksgiving, and we already have plenty of bookings for the month before Christmas. We even have a wedding to cater!"

"Three guests already? I thought you weren't open yet?"

"We have a couple here from Atlanta — just wait until you meet them! The Satterfields are delightful. Their daughter is married to the youth pastor at our church, plus they have business ventures in the area. They expect to stay with us regularly. There really isn't anything else in Jewel Lake that meets their expectations."

Didn't sound like any youth-pastor in-laws Pam had ever met, but whatever. "And the other guest?"

"Retired military, here for a few months to visit his daughter and grandkids. I couldn't very well refuse to have one of the rooms booked for three months solid!"

"No, of course not." Pam turned thoughtfully, noting the Christmas-themed potholders and towels. If that was all the decorating Julia had done in the kitchen, Pam could count herself truly blessed. She smiled at Julia. "Staff quarters?"

"In the walkout basement. Let me show you." Julia tugged her arm.

Pam let her hand glide along the stainless-steel counter, strangely reluctant to leave her new domain. She knew from experience she'd be spending at least half her waking hours in here, even if the dining hall was only open five evenings a week and someone else was handling breakfast.

"Oh, hi, Granger! Let me introduce you to our chef, who just arrived!"

Granger? A name Pam had never heard before an hour ago. It couldn't be... She turned toward the dining hall to see the tall, angular man from the Golden Grill beside Julia.

His gaze shifted to her, and his eyes widened.

She recovered first. "Granger? I'm pleased to meet you. I'm Pam Whorley, a friend of Julia's since our college days." She held out her hand.

He wrapped both his hands around hers, his blue gaze intense. "I'm happy to meet you... again."

"And, um, thank you for paying for my lunch. That wasn't at all necessary, but it was a nice gesture."

"You're welcome. It was the least I could do after Oliver—"

"You two have met?" Julia's gaze swung from one to the other.

Pam felt a sigh of relief to have the moment broken as she pulled free. She didn't dare shake her fingers out, though the temptation was strong. "He was at the diner."

"Oliver bumped her and sent her soup flying."

"Oh, no!" Julia's hand covered her mouth.

"It's all good." Pam forced a smile. "Now, you were going to show me to my quarters?"

"Can I bring in your bags, ma'am?"

Pam kept her smile in place as she looked back at Granger. "I'll handle them in a minute."

"That would be great, Granger. Here's a key to the elevator."

And Pam couldn't even kill her friend with her daggered eyes. What she really did not need was to see this man every single day for the rest of the year. At least, his rambunctious grandchildren weren't likely to make an appearance. She could only hope.

Granger stared after the two women as they walked toward the Employees Only sign on the door beside the grand staircase. This elevator led to the lower level, requiring a key or code for access, neither of which he had because, of course, he was a guest and not a staff member.

Julia had been thinking ahead, though. The elevator would allow him to use one of the luggage trolleys and haul Pam's belongings down in just a few easy trips. His knee would thank him.

He headed back outside, breathing deeply of the crisp autumn air. He wasn't going to get tired of Montana anytime soon. If only he could afford to lodge at Maranatha indefinitely, but the rate was a little steep for that. He'd settled on a three-month stay. It would give him long enough to see how his relationship with his daughter and her kids worked out.

Melissa was basically a stranger, except she looked a bit like Granger's sister and had a few of her mannerisms. At least Denise hadn't poisoned their daughter against him. Instead, she'd ignored the fact that Grant wasn't Melissa's father. Melissa had been nearly an adult before Denise had set the record straight with her.

Granger valued honesty. Clarity. He couldn't condone Denise's subterfuge, but he hadn't been consulted. All he could do was make lemonade with the lemons he'd been given. And lemon muffins and lemon-meringue pie.

He blinked away the vision of citrus dancing in front of his eyes and focused on the gray Altima with South Carolina plates in the parking area. He wouldn't have pegged Pam as Southern, though she had a hint of a drawl, now that he thought about it.

The car was unlocked, so he loaded boxes onto the trolley and pushed it back inside. He navigated it into the elevator then out on the lower level, pausing a moment to gain his bearings in this unfamiliar space.

Ah. Voices. He followed the sounds to a suite about double the size of his third-floor guest room. The living area had a small kitchenette in one corner, and he could see a bathroom and a bedroom through two open doorways.

"Granger! That was quick." Julia smiled as she turned to him. "If you'll just unload those over by the window, Pam can settle in at her leisure."

"Sure. Looks like another couple of loads." He dared a glance at Pam. What would it take to get an actual smile out of her? Not one that she felt compelled to offer because of social niceties?

"Thank you, Granger."

"You're welcome." What was he doing again? Right. Offloading the cart. Going for more. He'd be back here before he knew it. Maybe he could linger with the last load.

What on earth, Granger Durand?

This wasn't like him. Not even remotely. He'd been totally immune to womanly charms since his last furlough home with Denise, the visit when Melissa had been conceived, several months before the Dear John letter. He'd simply focused on his career, female soldiers around him notwithstanding. He'd met plenty of women over the years, and none had caught his attention for 30 seconds.

Why now?

Ears flaming, he shifted the boxes and got out of there as quickly as his knee would allow. He caught his breath leaning against the wall in the elevator.

Why now, indeed? If he were going to conjure up a recipe for his perfect woman, ingredients like faith and joy and humor would be the major components. He didn't have a read on Pam's belief system, but the other traits were nowhere to be found.

Maybe he could be the one to put a smile on her face. Now, where had that notion come from?

Julia. She was the type of woman he should be looking for though, from what she'd said, her husband had only been gone a couple of years. But it didn't matter, not to him, as he had nothing but a pleasant regard for Julia. In the two weeks he'd been a guest at the inn, he'd never once wondered if she might be ready to date.

He'd known for certain he wasn't.

And yet... why was he so sure? Because, suddenly, he wasn't. Not at all.

CHAPTER
Three

Wendy!" Pam squealed as her longtime friend set down her duffel bag and opened her arms. "I've missed you."

"I've missed you, too." Wendy hugged Pam tightly, nearly engulfing her as they rocked from side to side.

Wendy had never been slender, but she'd put on weight since Pam last saw her. She'd obviously reacted to her grief with her cheating husband the opposite way Pam had responded to the loss of her family. Pam had barely eaten. Didn't seem like that had been Wendy's modus operandi.

"Is Audrey here, too?" Pam looked past her friend.

Wendy rolled her eyes. "She is. Honestly, I should have driven myself from Oregon, but I didn't think my old van would make it. After spending two entire days with Audrey... well, I'm not sure how this scheme of Julia's is going to work."

"Aw, I'm sorry it was rough. You guys were best friends as kids."

"We haven't seen much of each other in recent years. She's always on me about my health, and she had plenty of time to make her case on the trip."

Pam's loyalty was torn, because Audrey had a point... but

maybe jumping straight into incrimination with someone you hadn't been in touch with for a long time had not been her brightest move. That was Audrey, though. She'd never been shy about expressing her opinions.

Some women could carry excess weight and look healthy. Wendy's skin was blotchy and puffy. But Pam was definitely not going to nag at the woman who'd introduced her to Audrey and the others back in Bible college. Wendy's habits and health were none of Pam's business.

"Talking about me?" Audrey breezed into the staff lounge on the inn's lowest level with Julia behind her. The glance she gave Wendy before turning to Pam was cool. "Pammy! You're looking good."

Had that been meant as another dig against Wendy? Oh, boy. Had Julia thought this reunion through?

"Thanks. You, too!" Pam meant it. Audrey's leggings and knit tunic showed off her tall, lean body.

"Hey, I'm here, too!" Christina entered the room to receive her own round of hugs. "Welcome, friends!"

Julia looked around in satisfaction. "Now we're just missing Laura. Last I heard, she'd be here Wednesday. I'm so excited!"

"Me, too!" Pam replied, since no one else seemed ready to echo their hostess and employer. It looked like Julia thought of them as a team, not as subordinates, which would be helpful, but if Audrey and Wendy were already at odds, and Chris had always been on the fringes, it looked like it was up to Pam to bridge the gap. "Is everyone hungry? Julia and I have put together a light meal while we all catch up."

The kitchen wouldn't open to the public for a couple of more days, but meanwhile, they needed to eat.

"Sounds good. I'm starved!" Wendy turned away from Audrey.

"I could handle something light," Audrey agreed.

Pam exchanged a glance with Julia. She'd have to let their host know about the rift later, though Julia might figure it out on her own before then.

"Chris?" Pam reached for her friend. "I know you're living at the old farmhouse, but you'll join us, right? Tonight and often?"

"Tonight, yes. Often? I'm not sure. It's a busy time of year out on the tree farm."

"Really?" Audrey asked. "I would think there wasn't much to do before you start selling trees at Thanksgiving."

Chris gave Audrey a tight smile. "You'd be wrong. We have 20 acres of evergreens. It's not a part-time job."

Had Chris been jabbing at Audrey's operation of the on-site spa and exercise facilities? Julia hadn't planned that as a 40-hour-a-week position.

Pam was going to get migraines if she felt like she needed to be the mediator in her friend group. They were all adults. Had been for 30-some years now. Was it too much to ask they all acted like it?

She led the way back to the dining room. Julia had set a table for the five of them earlier, while Pam had created a simple repast of a chef salad with sun-dried-tomato focaccia. Hopefully, it would satisfy everyone, unless Audrey had decided to become a vegetarian since their last reunion.

They gathered around the table, and Julia beamed, though she dabbed tears from her eyes. "Let me ask God for His blessing."

Pam ducked her head along with everyone else.

"Beloved Father, I am so grateful to You for lifelong friends and for traveling mercies. I pray that You will be present here at Maranatha Inn in a way that our guests will be able to feel, and that you will refresh our friendships with each other. Thank You so much for Pam's expertise in the kitchen, and I ask You to bless this food to our bodies. We love You. In Jesus's name, amen."

Pam picked up her fork to spear a chunk of hard-boiled egg.

"Hello, ladies. I'm sorry to interrupt but, Julia, may I speak with you a moment?" Granger Durand stood a few feet away, a smile in place.

Julia laid her napkin on the table as she rose. "Of course. But may I introduce my friends? Ladies, this is Granger Durand, who will be our guest until the end of the year, unless we can convince him to stay longer. Granger, you've already met Chris and Pam."

Granger nodded at them. Was it Pam's imagination, or did his gaze linger on hers for an extra few seconds? Not that she cared.

"Beside Pam is Wendy," Julia went on. "She'll be offering all sorts of creative activities for our guests and the community. I hope there will be something of interest to you as well!"

"Welcome to Jewel Lake, Wendy." Granger offered a smile.

"And beside Wendy is Audrey. The two of them were best friends as kids! I'm so glad they widened their circle to include the rest of us at Gilead Bible College. Audrey is a nutritionist and personal trainer. We'll soon have our fitness room available to all our guests."

"Sounds good. I was hoping to be able to lift weights closer than the gym downtown."

Audrey beamed at him. "Coming soon, Mr. Durand. I look forward to working with you."

Pam just bet she did. And that feeling in her own chest? Was absolutely not jealousy. Just because she'd met Granger first — well, after Julia and Chris — didn't mean she had any claim on him. She didn't even want one.

Go for it, Audrey.

But Granger's gaze connected with Pam's for a lingering moment before he stepped aside to speak with Julia.

It didn't mean a thing.

"What can I help you with, Granger?" Julia cast a glance back at the table surrounded by her friends.

He felt like a heel pulling her away. "I'm sorry. This is bad timing. I just wanted to let you know the hot water tap in my bathroom sink won't stop dripping. I could dig into it if you prefer not to call someone, but you still should know."

"Thank you for telling me. I'll call Steve's Plumbing. Hopefully he can send someone out quickly. There really shouldn't be a problem, since those were all just installed this past summer."

Granger nodded. "I agree. But still, if you need me to get in there…"

Julia waved her hand dismissively. "No, of course not. You're our guest. I'll get right on it. If Steve is going to be long, I'll move you to a different room."

"You're busy with your friends." Granger cringed. Had he made it sound like she was simply a socialite, not a business owner?

"My friends and business partners," she corrected with a smile.

He glanced at the group just as Pam's gaze slipped away from him. No, he'd probably imagined that. Had he, though? Did he want her to notice him? He'd been fine on his own for 35 years. He didn't need a woman complicating his retirement years.

Complicating or complementing? He shook his head slightly. Not a thought spiral he wanted to get into. "I'm headed down to the church to chat with Pastor Marshall. Do you need anything picked up in town?"

"Bless you, Granger. I don't think so."

"Well, let me know if you do." Granger turned back to the group. "Nice to meet you all."

"The pleasure is all ours."

Audrey, right? He'd have to keep an eye on that one.

Granger made good his escape, and a few minutes later, he strolled into the foyer of Creekside Fellowship. He was a few minutes early, so he paused to listen to the worship team's practice up on the platform.

Caleb Grant sang into the microphone as he strummed his

guitar. He nodded to Granger and kept singing "What a Beautiful Name."

Where was the drummer? Maybe she hadn't been able to make practice. But this song sure cried out for a solid beat. Granger's fingers tapped against the back of the last pew in the sanctuary.

Caleb stopped and discussed a bridge with the pianist before turning to the nearly empty building again. "Hey, you wouldn't happen to know your way around a drum set, would you? Casey broke her wrist, so we'll be without for a while."

Granger blinked. "Uh… I've toyed around with snares a few times."

"Really? Get up here and show us what you can do!"

He should have kept his mouth shut. On the other hand, hadn't he been praying for ways to get involved in the church community? That was the purpose of his appointment with Pastor Marshall. He glanced at his watch. "I have a meeting with the pastor in ten minutes."

Caleb grinned. "That's long enough. If you're willing, at least."

"Sure." Granger shook out his fingers as he walked toward the platform. He was so out of practice that he'd probably make a bad showing, but maybe it was like riding a bike. A man could hope.

He lowered himself to the drum throne, but the seat was at an uncomfortable height. Granger quickly adjusted it before settling back into position and picking up the drumsticks. He did a quick rat-a-tat-tat over the toms and hit the crash cymbal before meeting Caleb's eye. "What are you looking for here?"

The younger man demonstrated the beat, and Granger picked it up, adding a flourish here and there. Felt good. It had been ages.

At the end of the run-through, Caleb gave him a thumbs-up. "Are you willing to fill in for a few weeks? Because you'd be a lifesaver."

Was this Granger's answer? Or at least one of them? "Yeah, I'd be honored. It's been a while, but I could get back into it."

"I don't think you've lost your touch. Sounded good."

"Thanks. I should meet with Pastor Marshall now."

"We'll still be here when you're done, most likely."

Maybe he should cut the appointment short, or postpone it. Hadn't he come here to find purpose? It might not have required a meeting with the pastor to accomplish that goal, but he still needed to check in.

The receptionist looked up at his approach. "Come right in. Pastor Marshall is expecting you."

"Thanks, Mrs. McDiarmid."

"Melanie to you, Mr. Durand."

He grinned as he tapped on the pastor's door. "You got me there."

"Come in, Granger!"

Granger poked his head into the study. "I might need to rebook this appointment."

The heavyset man's eyebrows tipped up. "But you're here now."

"Right." Granger chuckled. "I told you on the phone I wanted to talk about volunteer options, but as I was coming into the building, Caleb asked if I could play the drums. Turns out he needs a drummer, and I can do that, so maybe that's my answer right there."

Pastor Marshall chuckled. "God's like that, isn't He? I'm sure you can make a difference right there on the worship team, but I do have a few possibilities I'd like to chat with you about. Check with Melanie about a new meeting time, or we could get together at the Copper Carafe for breakfast one morning in a more casual setting."

Why did Granger's brain slide through the fact that he'd seen Pam at breakfast the past few mornings, though it wasn't her shift to cook? He could hardly wait to try one of her entrees, if Julia hadn't talked her friend's cooking up too much.

It wasn't like he needed to make an excuse to see Pam. He wasn't looking for a relationship, remember?

Yeah, he remembered, all right. He didn't have the greatest

track record. Never mind that his romantic entanglements were in the distant past. *Far* distant past.

He shoved the thoughts aside and studied the pastor, a man of similar age to him. "Sure. You name the morning, and I'll be there."

Marshall perused his calendar. "Thursday at eight?"

"Sounds good."

"Excellent. Now go make my head worship leader happy."

"Will do." More to the point, Granger's desire was God's favor. And maybe it wouldn't hurt for Pam to see him taking a community role.

Not that he was thinking about her.

CHAPTER

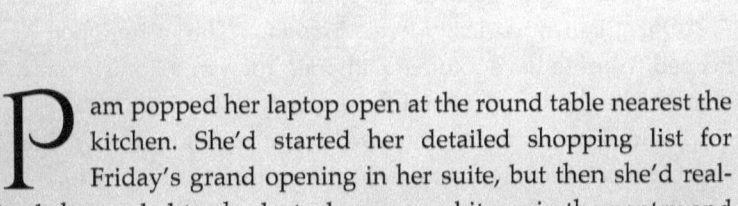

Four

P am popped her laptop open at the round table nearest the kitchen. She'd started her detailed shopping list for Friday's grand opening in her suite, but then she'd realized she needed to check stock on several items in the pantry and walk-in refrigerator.

It wouldn't do for her to miss a single ingredient for the planned seven-course dinner. Jewel Lake didn't sport a service that would make an immediate delivery like in Charleston. Also, the Super One downtown might not have everything she needed. It had been a while since she'd stocked a commercial kitchen from scratch, and never in a small town.

Hmm. She'd already ordered most of the key ingredients. She scrolled down the menu, making note of the most minuscule items.

Someone cleared a throat, and she looked up in surprise. "Granger! Hello."

"I'm sorry. I didn't mean to startle you."

"No worries. I was lost in my own little world."

"A foodie world?" Grinning, he gripped the back of the chair across from her.

Pam smiled. "Always. Don't trust anyone who says there's more to life than food."

Granger chuckled. "I'm guessing that leaves a lot of folks I shouldn't trust."

"Most likely." She studied him. "I meant to tell you your drumming sounded good in church yesterday."

"Thanks. I'm way out of practice, but it was kind of fun. The regular drummer broke her wrist."

"Good for you stepping in."

He shrugged. "I have little else on my schedule these days. My grandkids are in school, and my daughter isn't sure if she actually wants me in her life. Besides, she's working."

"Oh?" Pam's curiosity was piqued. "The coffee pot just beeped. Want to have a coffee with me? You can tell me about it." And maybe she'd understand those rowdy kids a little better.

"I didn't mean to interrupt what you're doing. I only didn't want to ignore you and walk right past without saying hello."

"But… coffee."

He held up both hands. "You got me there. If you're sure I won't take up too much of your time."

"I could use a break. What do you take in yours?" She closed her laptop.

"Just black, thank you."

"A man after my own heart." Pam's eyes widened as a flush ran up her neck and exploded across her face. "I meant about the coffee."

Granger grinned. "I knew what you meant. Maybe I could get it?"

"No, I'm good." Pam fled into the kitchen and poured two mugs. Then wiped up the spill from her trembling hands. Whatever was going on with her? She couldn't possibly find the man attractive, could she? Well, he *was* good-looking. Tall, lean, a gorgeous head of salt-and-pepper hair, short beard, and those intensely blue eyes.

She composed herself, plated two banana chocolate chip muffins, and carried out a small tray.

"Oh, what have we here?"

"Just some muffins I threw together earlier."

"You're spoiling me."

"No more than I'm spoiling myself." Pam offloaded the tray and retook her seat across from him. Now what? She couldn't remember the last time she'd invited a man to enjoy a break with her.

Granger took a sip. "So, you and Julia and the others go way back?"

"We were in Bible college together years ago. Then life happened and we spread to all corners of the country. We've only seen each other a few times since graduation. And that's been a while."

"And none of you are married now?" He held up a hand. "Sorry, that might be too personal a question."

"I'm widowed, as are Julia and Audrey." Pam bit her lip, trying to keep her tone light. "Chris was never married. Wendy is divorced. So is Laura, but you haven't met her yet. She's due in tomorrow."

"Life can be hard." He broke a piece off the muffin and popped it in his mouth. "Wow. This is really tasty."

"Thanks." Talk about awkward. "How about you? Is there a Mrs. Durand? You've mentioned your daughter…"

Granger grimaced. "My marriage was over almost before it began. Denise decided she didn't want to be a military spouse, after all. She sent divorce papers while I was overseas. Said she was remarrying, and her new husband would be our unborn child's father."

Pam stared at him. "You're kidding. How could anyone be that low?"

"That's Denise. And it's why I don't know my daughter, Melissa, very well. Or her kids."

"I'm sorry." And it explained a lot about the chance meeting in the Golden Grill.

He shrugged. "I let it happen. I'm paying for it now."

"It must have been very hard." She couldn't read his facial expression.

Finally, he said, "Without Jesus in my life, I would probably have just let it go completely. But He wouldn't let me keep taking the easy way."

What on earth was he saying? That he wouldn't have sought his daughter out? How could any man be like that? Pam held her coffee cup in front of her face. Maybe her response would be hidden.

"Those kids, though," Granger mused. "Their dad left them a couple of years ago. They're a mess, and they need a man in their life. Even more, they need God. They're more open to that than Melissa is."

Those kids did need Jesus, but Pam managed not to blurt the words. "I had children that age." Wait, what? No! She never announced that to strangers. Never. She surged to her feet. "I should get to work." But her work was in the closed laptop on the table in front of her.

Granger's gaze was even. "Had?"

"Killed in the same crash that took their father," Pam whispered.

Compassion shone in his blue eyes. "I can't even imagine."

"Be glad of that." She gulped for air. It was her turn to cling to the back of a chair. "Worst day of my life."

"I'm so sorry." Granger hesitated. "What were their names? Tell me about them?"

Now he wanted her to casually chat about them? It had been so long since she'd opened that compartment in her heart, even a little. Could she even manage words? And why should she? Now? To him?

"Courtney was twelve, Roderick ten."

Granger's heart clenched at Pam's tortured eyes. "The same ages as Sidney and Oliver." He closed his eyes, trying to imagine her loss, but the depth of it was beyond his comprehension. He'd lost buddies in Afghanistan. He'd seen kids die horrific deaths. His nights were still sometimes haunted by the memories.

How much more must Pam feel for her own children?

"I'm sorry. I shouldn't have pried."

"I don't even know why I told you that. I don't talk about them." She gulped for air.

It might be therapeutic.

But he managed to keep the words inside. He certainly didn't have the right to psychoanalyze her. "If you want to sometime, I'm here. I'll listen."

"Thanks." Her smile, more like a grimace, was so fleeting he might have imagined it.

Granger picked up the muffin and had another bite. "This is great. Moist. I love the banana chunks."

Slowly, she sank back into her chair.

He mentally pumped his fist. She hadn't fled, though she'd certainly been poised to do so. "So, I play the drums. Do you play an instrument?" Why did he feel the need to keep talking? Maybe he should just head down to the waterfront the way he'd meant to 20 minutes ago.

"I played the clarinet in high-school band and haven't picked it up since."

"Did you bring your instrument to Montana?"

"No. I sold it eons ago."

Granger searched for a new conversation starter. "How did you get into commercial cooking?"

Was that a look of relief she shot him? Maybe this was worth it. He couldn't leave while she was in the depths of despair. Bringing a woman to tears, even inadvertently, then walking out wouldn't be very kind of him. He was just being a nice guy. That was all.

Keep telling yourself that, Durand.

Okay, fine, he would.

"My parents owned a restaurant, so I was in the biz from childhood. But I wanted something more upscale than a franchise like theirs." She lifted a slight shoulder. "I went to Bible college then culinary school. Started a catering business, sold it, then cooked in a couple of prestigious restaurants. That's it."

He'd be willing to bet there was a whole lot more to her career path than she'd revealed, but he didn't need to know it. Not at this stage, anyway.

Granger blinked. There wouldn't be another stage beyond acquaintance. They were both at the inn temporarily. Rumor had it she'd return to South Carolina, and he wasn't sure what he was doing yet. Maybe looking for a house in Jewel Lake. An older man on his own could make do with an apartment, but he liked a little more elbow room, if possible. Sharing a home with Melissa and the kids was out of the question.

"Hey, is there more coffee?"

Granger looked up to see Audrey standing beside the table, eyeing him. Oh, boy.

"Sure is," Pam responded. "Muffins are in the walk-in."

"Great! Don't go anywhere. I'll be right back."

He shook his head as she sashayed away then caught Pam's grin. "What?"

"She's not very subtle."

It had been years since a woman had pursued him, not that Audrey had taken it that far. She probably wouldn't. She was just a friendly sort. Right? "I'm not interested in her."

"Looks like she'll do her best to get you to change your mind."

"It won't make any difference."

Pam's eyebrows arched. "You're a love-at-first-sight kind of guy? If there's no spark in the first meeting, there never will be?"

He opened his mouth, thought better of it, and closed it again. Was he a romantic? How else could he explain the instant draw he'd felt to Pam, even in the diner? "I've never wondered before. Do *you* believe in love at first sight?"

"Instalove?" She shook her head with a rueful grin. "Nothing lasting can come out of instant attraction. Slow and steady will win the race every time."

But would it? His marriage to Denise had been impulsive. That was hard to deny. It was also nearly 40 years ago. Had he really not changed a bit in all that time? If there was going to be a next time — and that was a huge if — he'd take it slow and easy and be really sure.

Why was he even putting an 'if' in there? He'd never once in all the intervening years felt inclined to pursue a relationship. Once burned, twice shy, had been his motto.

Audrey took a seat at the table, her hands cradling her mug. "So, what are you two deep in conversation about?"

Granger was not touching that with a ten-foot pole. "A bit of this and a bit of that."

She looked between them. "Am I interrupting something?"

Pam's response was quick. "No, of course not. I was working on Friday's menu and took a break when Granger came through. I really should get the details finalized so I can source the last few ingredients. I suspect I'll have to drive into Missoula for some items."

Audrey nodded. "The fitness room is open now, Granger. Vance Satterfield checked out the treadmill earlier. Loretta looked aghast that I might think she'd be interested in working out."

Granger laughed. He'd had breakfast with the couple from Atlanta quite a few times over the past few weeks. They were here visiting their daughter and son-in-law as well as checking on some of their investments. He'd found Loretta quite charming, but he could just imagine her response to Audrey. Too bad he'd admitted in her hearing that he'd been a regular at the downtown gym. If he didn't keep that knee flexed, it would seize right up on him.

Audrey turned to Pam. "You should come work out with me."

"I don't exercise. Thanks, anyway."

"You don't? But how will you keep your muscle mass as you age? You're not getting any younger, you know. You need a lot of protein and weight-bearing exercise to maintain your current fitness level. Even more if you need to build it back up."

Pam gave Audrey what Granger had always considered to be the 'mom look.' "Did I ask for your advice?"

"No, but you should."

"Want me to start meddling in your life?"

Audrey crossed her arms. "I have nothing to hide."

"Neither do I."

Did Audrey know the details about Pam's family? Pam had said the women hadn't been in close contact over the decades, and he couldn't help guessing these two hadn't ever been the closest of the group.

Or... maybe Audrey had gotten more opinionated with age. Granger's mother certainly had lost her filter the older she got. She'd been gone for several years now, so at least he didn't still have to wonder what would come out of her mouth next.

Audrey was hardly old enough to have that excuse. The women had to be, what, in their early or mid-fifties? Not much younger than he was.

Pam rose to her feet and picked up her mug and plate.

Granger gulped the last of his coffee and stood. "Let me get these before I head downtown."

"Sure." Pam shot a look at Audrey. "I'll be in the kitchen focusing on the grand opening menu. You know where to find me if the inn is burning down, or something equally dire happens."

Granger forced the wannabe grin off his face. Things around Maranatha Inn had just become a whole lot more interesting.

CHAPTER

Five

S he's just pulling in!" Julia squealed. "Oh, I'm so excited!"
Pam looked over to the kitchen door. "Who, Laura?"
"Of course, Laura. Who else? Santa Claus?"

Pam grinned and dried her hands on her apron. "Now, wouldn't that be a surprise?" Maybe Santa would make a jollier addition to their crew than Laura, or it could be that Audrey's forceful nature had made Pam leery of reconnecting with their other friend, who'd always seemed bigger than life. They'd had their factions in Bible college, but the past few days had proved that they'd all changed since those days. Become more set in their ways. They were the same people at their cores, yet intensely more.

Was that true of her, too? Hmm.

Pam followed Julia through the dining room to the foyer. Wendy and Audrey stood on the stoop outside with plenty of room for a hurricane to sweep between them. A compact white car with Maine plates came to a stop, and Laura erupted from the driver's seat with a dramatic curtsy. "Let the party begin!"

They swarmed around her, edging each other for hugs. As Pam expected, Audrey then linked arms with Laura and dragged her toward the staff elevator, with Julia on the other side.

Pam looked at Wendy and chuckled. "Some things never change."

"Yeah." Wendy bit her lip. "For instance, how come I'm still the only fat one of the bunch?"

"I wouldn't worry about it." Pam was concerned for her friend's health, but she wasn't going to turn into a second Audrey. "Be yourself."

Wendy looked down and fingered the hem of her top. "I'm not sure I want to be me. I wasn't good enough for Dave. Did I tell you who he left me for?"

Was this necessary? It had happened, what, three or four years ago? Maybe it was therapeutic for Wendy. "Tell me."

"A girl barely older than Adriel with a bikini bod. No wonder I couldn't keep him. Look at me."

"Wendy." Pam put her hands on her friend's shoulders. "Dave made his choices, and they didn't have anything to do with you."

"How can you say that? I was his wife. I should have been meeting all his needs, but I guess my fat body turned him off."

"It's on him, hon. Truly." Just as Mark had made choices that pulled him away from Pam. And, okay, fine, Pam had made choices, too. Their rocky marriage had been on both of them.

"Thanks for trying to make me feel better, but I don't. Even my kids barely want me around. That's why I came when Julia called. I told Faith about the invitation and that I wouldn't accept because of her — she's still in high school, you know — and she said go for it, she'd just move in with her dad. She wanted to try public school, anyway."

"Ouch."

"Yeah. So can you blame me for blaming myself?" Tears puddled in Wendy's eyes.

Pam wasn't the huggy sort, but she'd make an exception for Wendy. The poor woman needed a nonjudgmental friend. Her usual thought would be to offer food, but that might not be the best choice given Wendy's weight and self-esteem issues. But maybe that was judgmental on its own? Aargh, it was hard to know. "Hey, I have half an hour. Want to walk over to Chris's with me and see the Christmas tree farm?"

"How far is it?"

"Not far at all." Pam pointed to the lane that carried on beyond the inn's parking area. "Just around a few curves."

"I don't have on the right shoes."

Pam looked down at Wendy's flat sandals. "Those will be fine. It's not like we'll be mountain climbing."

Wendy shuddered. "Whew. I guess I can give it a try."

"I've only been here a few days longer than you, but I've only been up there once. Chris invited Julia and me for lunch early on."

"She doesn't come by the inn much."

"No, she says it's pretty busy getting the trees ready for sale."

"That doesn't even make sense." Wendy fell into step beside her as they ambled toward the lane. "Don't the trees grow themselves?"

Pam chuckled. "Apparently, it's a whole thing. Chris will be happy to tell you all about it if you ask nicely." Which Audrey hadn't, the other day.

They entered the grove of evergreens. "It smells nice in here," Wendy commented.

"It does. I don't know why I don't walk out here more often. It's not like I don't have any time for it. I get in my own ruts, I guess."

"I understand."

The lane wound up a slight rise. Already, Pam could hear Wendy's breath puffing, so she stopped to look around. A distant neigh caught her attention. There was a horse stable next door, closer to town, but she'd never heard a horse up here before.

She spotted a rocky knoll on the hillside overlooking the tree farm and touched Wendy's arm. "Look! Horses."

Wendy's eyes grew wide. "Are they wild?"

"No. See, there are people, too. I'm sure they're from Happy Trails. Julia mentioned they'd be building a picnic shelter up there next summer."

"Interesting. I've never been on a horse, and I suppose that's not going to change anytime in the foreseeable future. Are you a rider?"

"No. Maybe someday, but not so far."

Wendy looked up the lane. "How much farther to Chris's?"

"Not far now." Maybe dragging Wendy out here had been a mistake, but how could it be? They were staying in such a beautiful area, full of God's nature. Surely, they should experience it, at least a little.

The tension eased a tiny bit in Pam's heart. She had a lot to be thankful for. She knew it, but sometimes it was so hard to remember. Seeing Granger's grandkids the other day had boomeranged her back a dozen years, and it had been hard to recover from that.

"Do you think you'll ever marry again?" Wendy huffed for breath.

Until the past few days, the thought hadn't even crossed Pam's mind, but then there'd been that weird little conversation with Granger about love at first sight. Which was a totally ridiculous notion. She might have fallen hard for Mark quite quickly but, in retrospect, that was an argument *against* instalove, not for it. It hadn't taken long for the fractures to appear in their marriage, though they'd done their best to hide them from anyone else as long as they could. Even their parents hadn't had a clue.

"Pam?"

"I doubt it," Pam said at last. "Marriage was all of our dreams in Bible school—"

"They don't call it bridal school for nothing. We were all looking for our M.R.S. degrees."

"Right. Even Chris seemed to be looking for someone back then, but she never met him. Maybe she had the right of it, not settling for a few temporary tingles."

Wendy sighed deeply. "I don't want to marry again, either. Not that anyone would want me."

Here they went again, and Pam didn't feel like she was in a

healthy enough place herself to counsel her friend. Not that Wendy was asking for advice. Was she?

"I hear Chris's chainsaw. Let's get moving."

Granger had kept his early morning habit of swinging by the gym in downtown Jewel Lake. While it was nice that the inn's fitness facility was now open to guests — he'd popped in to have a peek — he wasn't interested in hanging out in Audrey's presence. She seemed a little too eager for his liking.

No, if he were going to seek out a woman to spend time with, it would be Pam Whorley. Not that he was going to follow through with that initial attraction. Actually, attraction was too strong a word. Call it awareness.

Her smile as they chatted in the dining room yesterday came to mind, very different from his first impression at the Golden Grill when she'd seemed grumpy. But then, Granger's grandchildren truly hadn't made the best first impression. Those kids. How to be a presence in their life that helped ground and balance them? The societal image of an indulgent grandfather wasn't one he dared embrace.

Sidney and Oliver were the same age as Pam's kids had been when they died. He couldn't even begin to imagine the pain she'd endured, losing her entire family in an instant. No doubt, she'd had a great marriage and been a loving mother.

Pastor Marshall entered the Copper Carafe, and Granger forced his brain to shift gears. Their upcoming discussion would have to be more comfortable than thinking about a woman Granger had no intention of pursuing a relationship with.

The portly reverend lowered himself into the chair across from him, and a server hustled over with a thermal coffee pot. Ministers must get special treatment. Granger'd had to stand in line for his own brew.

"I hope you haven't been waiting long."

"Only a few minutes. How are you doing?" Because the man didn't look good.

"Just tired." Marshall pulled a white handkerchief from his pocket and mopped his sweating brow. "Can't seem to get healthy, you know? It's always one thing or another." He eyed Granger. "It must be nice to be retired."

"Yes? But sometimes it's also tedious. Hence why I wanted to talk to you about volunteering."

"Right. Right. Young Eli has a lot on his plate these days since I've been unwell."

'Young' Eli, Creekside's youth pastor, must be pushing 40. "I'm sorry to hear about your health struggles. Is taking a leave-of-absence an option?"

The man waved a hand. "I took a few months last year, but I'm still not back to speed. The doctors ran tests, but all they can tell me is that I should lose weight. Shouldn't everyone when they get to our age?" Then he looked Granger up and down. "Maybe not you."

"The military doesn't let a man get too soft." Granger would prefer to leave it at that. "I've always enjoyed working out, and now, with my bum knee, it's even more important to keep limber."

"I never understood the appeal. Might be too late for me now."

"Oh, I don't know. How old are you?"

"Sixty-two."

"You might be only two-thirds of the way through life."

Marshall blinked. "That's a point. But enough about me. I was telling you about Eli. He'd talked about hosting a gala type thing for Thanksgiving, reaching out to some of Jewel Lake's less privileged but, like I said, he's pretty stretched since he's covering for me so much. Do you know anything about running events like that?"

Whoa. Granger had raking leaves in mind, or maybe a few repairs around the building that didn't require trade licensing. Running events? Not so much.

"Eli thought about hosting a dinner. We have volunteers in the congregation who'd be happy to help cook and serve and decorate and all that. We just need someone to coordinate everything."

Hmm. Pam was a chef. Julia seemed an expert organizer.

But Granger was the one who'd expressed willingness to volunteer. He couldn't very well rope other people into it... although, why not? He'd picked up killer negotiating skills in the military. Plus, it might be fun to work with Pam on a community project.

Nope. Don't go there. But, again... why reject the idea out of hand? "Let me think on it a few days. Pray about it."

Marshall reached over the table and gripped Granger's forearm. "I knew I could count on you."

Granger chuckled. "I haven't agreed to anything yet."

"But you will. It's a good idea. Better yet, a God idea."

He wasn't going to let the pastor railroad him. "Have you done this other years? Any precedents or expectations?"

Marshall shook his head. "We talked a bit about it summer before last, but then my health took a nosedive, and Eli was barely keeping everything afloat. Some of the men of the church stepped in then to help with the youth group — they're still doing it, over a year later — but there was simply no bandwidth to expand at that time. But Eli mentioned it to me again a few days ago in our meeting. We asked God for a sign whether to proceed or not. We knew we needed help if that were to happen." He leaned back in his chair. "You, my friend, are an answer to prayer."

Granger laughed as he held up both hands. "God and I will need to have our own discussion about that. Don't jump to conclusions."

"You go ahead and chat with our Father. He has a heart for

reaching out to the needy folks in our community. We've got a lot of single parents struggling to make ends meet. It would be great to give them a nice meal and evening out. Eli figured to get some coupons and things to give out as well."

"Coupons? That means they still have to buy." Granger knew his daughter had chosen to do without some things since Chad left her and the kids. She had a job as a pharmacy assistant, but her budget only stretched so far, and the kids' needs came first.

"I see your point. There are details we'd need to work out, for sure." The good pastor's face brightened. "Have you ever played Santa Claus? We could personalize gifts for everyone. You could dress up and pass them out."

"You look more like Saint Nick than I do."

Marshall waved a hand. "Nothing a little padding on you wouldn't cure."

CHAPTER
Six

P am took a deep breath. Why was she so nervous? This opening night was nothing compared to the pressure at the Hydra in Charleston, but it meant a lot to Julia and the future of Maranatha Inn, and that mattered more.

The dining room was full of local dignitaries and their spouses, from the mayor to the pastors to the bank manager to the editor of the Jewel Lake Gazette. A few prominent businesspeople rounded out the group. These people, as a group, had the potential to influence the future of Maranatha Inn.

And it was Pam's job to impress them favorably.

She could do this. The guests were currently visiting over rosemary salted nuts, a selection of cheeses, and an assortment of crackers Pam had baked just yesterday. Mentally, she ran through the menu. She and Darla, her kitchen helper, had prepped everything they could earlier. Now it was a matter of clockwork.

Pam checked the time. She felt the familiar, welcome rush as she nodded at Darla. "Ready? It's go time!"

The other woman nodded firmly. "Ready."

The three young men hired to serve tonight stood attentively at the pass-through.

Pam caught Julia's eye where she sat at the nearest table with the inn's neighbor, Monte Newman, and his sister and brother-in-law, the Johannessons. Monte had been by the inn several times in the past week. Once he'd brought a couple of peach pies, and Pam had to admit the man was an excellent pastry chef. She'd asked Julia if there was anything going on, and Julia had smiled and shook her head. Monte had been a good friend of Julia's late husband, and now he was a good friend to her. Okay, then. Tell yourself what you need to hear.

Now Julia rose from her seat, looking every inch the owner of an elegant inn with her hair in an up-do that had taken Laura an hour to achieve. Julia's russet gown set the tone for autumn-themed decor. "I thank you all for coming this evening as we officially open Maranatha Inn. This was a long-time dream of my late husband, George, and me, and I'm only sorry he didn't live to see the culmination of all his hopes and plans. But God is still good."

A few amens as well as murmurs of sympathy sounded from around the dining room.

"I would like to invite Pastor Marshall Smith of Creekside Fellowship to ask the Lord's blessing on tonight's meal and conversation."

Pam tuned out the reverend's prayer as she and Darla ladled wild rice and kale soup into bowls and set them on the pass. The crudités for the next course were ready to pull from the walk-in, and the blueberry vinaigrette awaited the mussels.

She lost herself in the familiar rhythm of the kitchen. Darla was rarely out of step as they worked through the courses. A sorbet to cleanse palates came after the mussels, followed by locally sourced, roasted root vegetables and stuffed beef tenderloin. By the time the harvest salad course had been removed, and the pumpkin gingerbread cheesecake was ready to serve, Pam was buzzing with adrenaline.

They'd pulled it off!

Out in the dining room, Julia introduced her staff to the gathered dignitaries. Pam peeked in the mirror in the kitchen's powder room and adjusted her hair net beneath her chef's hat. She exchanged her apron for a clean one.

"And last, but definitely not least, I'd like you to meet our chef, Pamela Whorley, who launched the Hydra in Charleston, South Carolina, to Michelin-starred fame!"

Pam stood in the kitchen doorway as applause rolled across the dining room. She smiled and nodded.

As the ovation eased, Julia carried on. "She was aided in the kitchen this evening by Darla Reim and your esteemed servers, Sam, Nathan, and Dean. Thank you, all of you!"

The clapping was shorter this time.

"We welcome your dinner reservations Wednesday through Sunday evenings. We also invite you to choose Maranatha's Christmas Tree Farm for your holiday greenery this year. Also, Wendy Clarke will be hosting craft workshops on Saturdays for those who'd like to create your own wreaths, decor, and more. Our first such event, building a gingerbread house, will be held the first Saturday of November. If you're not signed up for our Maranatha Inn News weekly email, please consider subscribing. You'll be the first to know about our dinner specials and other events. Thank you all for coming!"

And may word-of-mouth enthusiastically spread the news that Maranatha Inn is open for business.

Pam retreated to the kitchen. She and Darla had been tidying behind themselves as much as time allowed, while the boys had done the same with the dishwasher. Now it was time for a concerted effort to put the kitchen to rights. After all, the morning cook would arrive early for breakfast prep and would rightly expect a pristine workplace ready for her creativity.

No shift was complete until the kitchen was clean. Out of habit, Pam glanced at the clock. They had an hour to go, at least.

Granger couldn't get the busy evening out of his mind. He'd resisted Julia's invitation to the dinner at first. He was just a visitor to Jewel Lake, not a community mover or shaker, but she'd persisted. His curiosity had gotten the best of him, and… wow.

The hype about Pam's culinary awards hadn't prepared him for the perfection of the seven-course dinner. Every morsel had exploded in his mouth, releasing delectable flavors.

Good thing he hadn't known cuisine like this existed when he'd enlisted in the military at 18, or he'd have never been able to subsist on army ration packs during their missions.

Pam had forever ruined his palate. Maybe she'd forever ruined more than that, because he hadn't been able to get her out of his mind before tonight, but now? His esteem for her had ticked up several enormous notches. She was all kinds of amazing.

And he could try to convince himself he wasn't sitting in the dimly lit lobby waiting for a glimpse of her exiting the kitchen, but it would be pointless to pretend. The three servers had headed out half an hour ago. The assistant had left about ten minutes back, but light still shone above and below the swinging doors. The cleanup noises had ceased.

Perhaps Pam was sitting in the quiet space, catching a breather. She must've been pretty pumped to keep that pace through seven perfect courses.

Granger should check on her.

Right? He rose from the leather love seat near the gas fireplace with its low, flickering flames. Just then, the main light went out, and he heard as much as saw Pam exiting the space.

"Hey, Pam." Better to speak than catch her completely by surprise.

"Who — Granger?"

"It's me. I just wanted to let you know what a fabulous job you did tonight. That was amazing."

She came closer on near-silent shoes. "You waited up to tell me that? It's nearly midnight."

"You sound tired. I'm sure you must be exhausted."

"I'm tired, but I'm also revved." The sound of her chuckle underscored both claims. "It will be a while before I can fall asleep."

"Did you eat?"

"I... I think so?"

Granger shook his head, not that she could clearly see him. "But you're not sure?"

"I had a few bites here and there. I'm not hungry."

"I, uh, grabbed a couple of protein shakes from my room's fridge. I thought you might like one."

"That's incredibly thoughtful. The idea of food on a fork doesn't sound at all appealing, but a filling drink sounds amazing."

He pumped his fist, and she laughed. So did he. "Come on, have a seat here by the fireplace. Relax for a few."

"Okay." She sat on the cushions facing the low flames.

Granger settled beside her and passed her a chilled bottle. "Strawberry cream. Hope that's okay."

"Sounds perfect." She twisted the lid off, took a sip, and leaned back. "How did the evening seem out there?"

"The food was incredible."

Pam chuckled, sounding tired. "Thanks, but I meant the rest of it. Did we impress all the right people?"

"It sure seemed like all the correct notes were struck. Quite a few of the visitors signed up for the weekly emails, at least. And, if I'm not mistaken, several tables were reserved for the next few evenings."

"Excellent."

"Do you ever get tired of being the chef? Is it hard to enjoy other people's cooking?"

She turned toward him. "It's a mix. I have to admit, I had low expectations that day in the Golden Grill. Their decor is so unbelievably tacky that I expected the fare to be tired and dated, as well."

Granger grinned at her. "But they blew you away, huh?"

"It was really good. Surprisingly so."

"I'm sorry again for my grandkids that day."

Pam shrugged. "It's okay. I'm sorry for my reaction. I was on edge and, well, it showed. I wasn't very gracious."

"So, I, uh, was wondering…" Granger cleared his throat and leaned his elbows on his knees. Here went nothing.

"Hmm?"

"You've got two nights off a week. Could I take you for dinner in Missoula one of those evenings?"

"Me?"

He made a show of looking around the quiet, dimly lit lobby. "I don't see any other exceptional ladies here. Yes, you."

Her gaze caught on his. "Are you asking me on a date?"

"Yes? But if you'd rather consider it dinner with a friend, I can live with that." For now.

Was he seriously considering getting romantically involved again? It seemed his heart was inclined that direction, but that didn't make it a good idea. She'd only committed to the inn for three months. What if she returned to South Carolina in the new year?

For that matter, he wasn't settled here, either. But wasn't his first responsibility to Melissa, Sidney, and Oliver? He couldn't just pack up and move to Charleston. Sure, long-distance relationships existed, but he was 59. He wasn't going to play that sort of game at this stage of his life. Been there, done that, got the papers in the mail.

"I'd like that," she said softly. "How about Tuesday?"

Granger's brain slid back to the present. "Perfect. I'll figure out a good place and make a reservation. Does that work for you?"

"Sure." Pam drank the rest of the protein shake. "Thank you. That really hit the spot."

He held out his hand, and she set the bottle in it, her touch grazing his palm. A flicker of awareness rippled through him. What would happen if he reached for her hand without the smoothie bottle in the way? Would she let him hold it? Would she return the gesture?

Man, he would have thought he was way beyond this kind of attraction. He'd be closing out his sixth decade soon. Weren't romantic tingles for teens?

Seemed not. Huh, who knew?

Pam yawned, covering her mouth with her hand. "Sorry. Part of my body is ready to give in to sleep, but my brain is still buzzing."

It wasn't Granger's mind whirring. It was every cell in his body. "I should let you go."

"I couldn't move right now if the inn were on fire."

Mixed messages, but it seemed like she wanted to stay here, with him, a bit longer. "Tell me about your hobbies. What do you like to do in your spare time?" He already knew that wasn't exercising or playing her clarinet, but surely there was more to her than cooking.

"I used to play soccer back in the day. I coached my daughter's team."

Granger couldn't have kept his hand to himself if it had been tied down... which it wasn't. He reached over and covered Pam's clenched fist with his. "I haven't been much for soccer — or any sport, really — since my knee."

She turned her hand over and laced their fingers together.

Granger forgot to breathe for a few seconds.

"What happened?"

"The typical Afghanistan war injury. A roadside bomb went off. Our vehicle turned into shrapnel. My leg was shattered." He swallowed hard. "Two soldiers died."

"I'm sorry."

"Yeah. Me, too." Granger stared into the flames. "They were good guys. They didn't deserve that end any more than I did. Stony had a wife and kids back in the States. I had nobody. I should have died instead of him."

"I don't think that's how it works," she said softly.

"It doesn't seem to." He shot a glance at her and focused on the warm pressure of her palm against his. She grounded him. "It took me a while to accept that God wasn't done with me yet."

"I know what you mean. Mark... Courtney... Roderick... they didn't deserve to die, either. Survivor's guilt is a real thing."

They had that in common, even though Pam had lost family members. The guys in his unit had been like family, though it wasn't exactly the same.

Pam's voice was quiet. "Did you ever figure out why God spared you?"

Granger shook his head. "Not really. For my daughter, maybe. I had a fulfilling teaching career after active duty. I'd like to think I made a difference, but any old fossil could have done what I did."

"I'm sure your unique experiences meant something to the students."

"Maybe." He caressed her fingers, loathe to leave the room, though it was getting late. "You?"

"Why did God spare me? I wasn't in the car with them. Mark was taking the kids to his parents' house so we could have a weekend getaway." She bit her lip.

Granger felt like a heel for asking. For pushing her to talk about her deceased husband and kids. Hadn't she said she *never* discussed them? But she seemed somewhat willing tonight. "I'm sorry."

"We'd hit a rough patch."

Her voice was so quiet he could barely pick out her words.

"We were going to try again. We never really got the chance, and I don't know if it would have worked out. We were two very different people, and I don't have any idea why I'm telling you all this. My friends don't even know that Mark and I separated for several months." Pam released his hand and surged to her feet.

Pam had segued so casually he barely caught the shift before she pulled away. He looked at her standing in front of him, clutching her arms around her middle. "Thank you for trusting me with that."

"You, too. But I should go." She stepped back, giving him enough room to stand without bumping into her.

Granger wanted to comfort her. Hug her. Kiss her.

Whoa.

Instead he touched her shoulder lightly. "Good night, Pam. I'll be praying for you."

She blinked a few times. "Thanks."

"And I'll let you know about our date, okay?"

"Okay." She pivoted on her heel, hurried over to the staff elevator, and punched in her code. Seconds later, the doors swished shut behind her.

Pam might be gone, but Granger was a goner.

And he didn't even mind.

CHAPTER
Seven

Pam had slept maybe five hours which, sadly, was about par for the course for her post-menopausal self. She'd lain awake staring at the ceiling reviewing not only the restaurant's opening night, but the fireside chat with Granger afterward.

Her brain had not been playing tricks on her over the past week and a half. He wanted to date her.

It might be only 5:30 am, but she slipped out of bed, into her one-piece swimsuit, and out the French door to the staff hot tub tucked beneath the main floor deck. She pressed the button to slide the cover off then the one that activated the jets before lowering herself into the steamy depths.

Ah.

A beautiful perk of working for Julia at Maranatha. One of many, if she were honest. Was she sure she wanted to leave at the end of the year? She'd only promised Julia three months and, if she were truly planning to leave, Julia should already be looking for a chef to step into Pam's shoes.

Into Pam's dream commercial kitchen. She'd designed it with Julia over the miles and over many months. It would likely also be some other chef's dream come true.

And then there was Granger. The situation seemed hopeful, but did she really deserve another chance at romance?

In hot water up to her chin, Pam closed her eyes and tilted her face upward. "God?" she whispered. "What am I supposed to do with this?"

The French door creaked slightly as it opened, and Pam sighed. So much for solitude... but it was doubtless one of her friends, so she'd put on a smile. Because that's what she always did.

Except when she stayed grouchy... but she was trying not to.

"Hi. That looks so inviting." Wendy sounded wistful.

Pam opened her eyes to see her friend standing nearby wrapped in a fluffy robe with a flannel nightgown peeking beneath its hem. "Come on in. The water's fine."

Wendy shook her head. "I don't have a swimsuit."

"We should go shopping later."

"No. I couldn't."

"Why on earth not?"

"No one wants to see my body like that." Wendy poked her toe at the edge of the hot tub.

"Hon..." Pam started gently. Where was she going with this? She didn't even know. "Dave's a jerk, you know that?"

A fleeting smirk crossed Wendy's face, gone so quickly Pam wasn't certain if she'd imagined it. "I prefer not to speak badly of Dave. I drove him to it."

"I can appreciate not wanting to start a flame war in front of your kids, but I'm your friend, and so are the others here. It's okay to name the problem. The problem is Dave. It is not you."

"It takes two."

And Pam knew that, all too well. She and Mark had both been at fault for their issues. She'd worked too many hours and brought her job's stresses home. Mark felt like he had to pick up all the slack, all while working long hours himself. Their offspring had turned into latchkey kids, and Courtney, especially, had been increasingly resentful.

If only Pam could go back and do those years again. Maybe she could have staved off their separation and those extra difficult months before they agreed to try again, this time with counseling.

If only they hadn't planned that particular marriage retreat, though. If only Mark hadn't driven the kids to his parents' house for the weekend. If only…

But there was no going back. They'd never had the chance to resurrect the dry bones of their marriage. Would they even have been successful? Since that awful day, Pam had clung to the belief that they would have made it. They'd have found their old passion and reignited it.

Wendy tightened her arms around her middle and turned to go back inside.

Pam had been lost in her own thoughts. "Wendy? Jump in in your skivvies. No one is going to know or care."

Her friend's eyes widened as her jaw slacked. "That's even worse!"

"We're going shopping this week. Not sure Jewel Lake will have swimsuits this time of year, but I'm sure we can find something in Missoula."

"It's October. And also, no."

"People go to Hawaii and on cruises or whatever all year around." Maybe Wendy was simply self-conscious about salespeople's judgment. "Or we could look online."

"Better. But still no."

"Wendy…"

"*Pam.*" Wendy glowered at her. "You couldn't possibly understand what it's like to be me."

Pam was on no health kick. Sure, she tried to cook healthy food and eat it in moderation. She liked to get outside for walks, but that was about the extent of it. Her job kept her on her feet. Maybe she was simply blessed with a great metabolism.

She shoved Audrey's knowing smirk out of her mind. If she couldn't even handle Audrey's opinions for herself, how much more must Wendy feel the barbs?

"Embrace who you are, my friend." Like Pam was such a good example of that.

Wendy looked down at her arms wrapped around her middle and chuckled. "Isn't that what I'm doing?"

"Ha." Pam grinned. "That's not what I meant, and you know it. It's an inside job, between you and God."

"He's punishing me."

"I don't think so, hon."

"Could you please get real?"

Pam straightened up, and her shoulders rose above the churning hot water. "You want me to jump on the bandwagon and castigate you for being overweight? How would that help?"

"I don't know, but I don't deserve you to be so nice about it or pretend it's not true."

Pam took a deep breath. "First of all, assuming what people think just gets you into trouble. If someone glances your way, they could just as easily be wishing they had your gorgeous hair or wondering where you got those cute boots. You're giving your perception of their unspoken thoughts too much power over you."

Wendy bit her lower lip.

But Pam was just getting warmed up. "Secondly, Dave's a jerk, and everyone knows that. But you're giving him power over your self-worth. People like him poke at other people because of how they feel about themselves. He tries to hide his own flaws by putting you down. The worst part is he's still controlling you."

Man, she'd like to do more than kick Dave where it would hurt most. Also, she had no idea how to help Wendy break this mentality. Maybe it wasn't her responsibility. She knew it wasn't, not really, but she couldn't help but try. They had once been so close, but they'd drifted apart due to years, busy lives, and distance.

"Wendy, here's the thing. You carry some extra weight. We all have things we perceive as physical flaws." This was not the time to mention the five pounds she'd recently added herself. Yay for menopause. "But that's not who you are. You're a beautiful person. You're kind. You have one of the most giving hearts I've ever known, always willing to help others. You're a precious child of God, and your body is just... your body. A shell that contains who you really are."

"Thank you," Wendy whispered, her eyes brimming with tears. "It's so hard. I know God loves me, but also, my body is His temple, and I've been a terrible temple keeper. I don't know how to get around that."

Getting Audrey involved was not an option, though their friend would rub her hands in glee and stalk Wendy's every step and every forkful. Like anyone needed that sort of legalism.

"How can I help you?" Pam asked carefully.

"I don't know." Wendy managed a tearful chuckle. "All I know is, it's not by serving me extravagant dinners every night. Last night was amazing, but way over the top."

"Seven-course dinners won't be a regular occurrence." And just like that, Pam's mind shot back to the fireside in the lobby after the main event. Would that be a regular occurrence?

Granger had somehow missed running into Pam all day yesterday. Oh, she'd been in the kitchen throughout the evening, but he wasn't going to interrupt her work hours. And waiting in the lobby after hours again had only seemed like a good idea for two minutes. Maybe that was a habit they'd get into in the future, but this thing between them was way too fragile for him to come across as stalking her.

Now he sat on Creekside Fellowship's platform tinkering with the drums while Caleb Grant led the congregation in worship. Granger's hands had no trouble playing along while his eyes wandered to the woman sitting toward the back of the sanctuary between Julia and Wendy. She sang along but, if her gaze caught on his, he couldn't tell.

"I will Sing of the Goodness of God" was a great song, maybe one he resonated with more the older he got. Had God been faithful all his life? Sure had, even when Granger hadn't been. Yes, he was going to keep singing of God's goodness that had pursued him all his days.

Practicing for the worship sessions had become meaningful. He'd immersed in the songs they were going to lead in a way he hadn't when the selections simply rolled past him on a Sunday morning. But now? He was deeply grateful for the opportunity to soak in the thought-provoking lyrics and let them challenge him.

After church, he was going to talk to Pam, though, even if he had to elbow his way past her friends. He'd booked a table at the Kaleidoscope for Tuesday evening, but he didn't have Pam's number to share the information. He'd ask for that, and maybe she'd be open to a quick lunch at the Golden Grill today. Although, Granger had noticed the diner was crowded at noon on Sundays. Maybe there was somewhere else.

The worship set ended, and Granger followed the other musicians off the platform to their seats near the front. Caleb's wife, Sage, slipped her hand into his when he settled beside her.

Would Pam sit up front and welcome Granger so naturally as time went on? Surely hand-holding in church wasn't simply the realm of kids Caleb and Sage's age. Uh… they were probably in their mid-30s and had a couple of youngsters of their own. Not kids, so much. Not anymore.

Granger listened as Pastor Eli presented the Word. The two pastors had been alternating Sundays as they preached through the fruits of the Spirit. Today's topic was faithfulness, and Granger's heart swelled at the thought of how God had always been there for him, even when he hadn't welcomed it. Had Pam felt the same through her own trials? He couldn't imagine the pain she'd been through, losing her family like that, especially when her relationship with her husband had been on eggshells at the time.

Finally, he resumed his place for the closing song and benediction. By the time they'd completed the postlude, the crew from Maranatha Inn had disappeared. Granger submerged his disappointment. He'd simply have to get Pam's number from Julia if he didn't see her later today.

He left the building a few minutes later to find Melissa leaning on the hood of his car in the nearly empty parking lot. Both kids were over on the playground, Oliver on the monkey bars, and Sidney watching with hands on her hips. "Hey, Dad."

"Hi, honey. Good to see you." Also, unusual. She let the kids attend with him some weeks, but hadn't come herself. "What's up?"

"I just found out that I have to go to a conference in Salt Lake City for work. Jason was supposed to go, but he's got the flu, so the pharmacy needs to send me instead."

Granger's heart stuttered. "You need me to watch the kids?"

"If you would?" Guarded hope shone in her eyes.

"Of course. That's why I'm in Jewel Lake. To be whatever you need from your old dad."

"Great. I'm catching the 6:20 flight out of Missoula, and I should be back Wednesday evening. Sidney has figure skating on Tuesday, and of course, they both have school every day. If I think of anything else you need to know, I'll make a note of it."

He blinked. "Today?"

"Yes, today. If the conference were later in the week, Jason might have recovered enough for him to go. But he isn't, so I need to."

"Okay." Granger's mind spun. It wasn't okay, not really. Not when he had a date with Pam on Tuesday — a date it seemed he'd need to cancel. Even if he wanted to take the children along for dinner — which he did not — Sidney's rink time interfered. He'd popped by the arena to watch her practice over the past few weeks. He'd just never thought he'd be the adult in charge of making it happen.

"Thanks, Dad." Melissa straightened away from the car. "I appreciate it. I need to leave for the airport by five, so if you could come over around four, we'll have time to get you up to speed."

"Okay. Sounds good. Don't worry about us. We'll be fine."

His daughter rolled her eyes. "Of course, you will be. It's not like they're toddlers anymore." She turned toward the playground and bellowed, "Kids!"

The two of them meandered over, not in any hurry to obey. Maybe Granger had been military too many years. He wanted them to jump, run, and salute.

"It's settled. Your grandfather will stay with you while I'm gone to Salt Lake. You two be good for him, okay?"

"Yay, Gramps!" Oliver slipped his hand into Granger's and beamed up at him.

Sidney snapped her gum and raised her eyebrows at him. She was a tough nut to crack, that one. "Yay." Distinct lack of enthusiasm.

"We'll have a great time!" Granger poured enthusiasm into his voice.

"We'll head home now and get ready. See you in a few hours." Melissa pointed at her car, and the kids clambered inside. A minute later, she sped away with a tap to her horn.

Granger stood in the parking lot beside his own car. Two big problems here. One, he could only hope Pam would understand his need to put his grandchildren first. And, two? He'd never in his life been the sole adult responsible for minors of any age. He could only hope he was up for it.

CHAPTER
Eight

P am's phone buzzed with an incoming text. So much for enjoying a little downtime before heading into the kitchen for her last shift of the week. When she'd checked earlier, only three tables had been booked. It was her job to wow those people so much they'd return and bring their friends.

She reached for her phone, sighing.

Julia: *Granger is in the lobby and wants to talk to you.*

Pam's heart soared like a helium-filled balloon cut loose from its mooring. Granger was about the only interruption she'd welcome at the moment. Where was he taking her on Tuesday? It had taken all her self-control not to search the internet for the top restaurants in Missoula.

Pam: *I'll be up in a minute.*

Julia: *Is something going on that I should know about? [heart eyes emoji]*

Hmm. It might be too early to clue her boss-slash-friend in. Pam would just ignore that question for now.

She checked her hair and makeup in her bathroom mirror and gave herself a stern talking-to. "Don't mess this up, Pamela Jean Whorley. He's a great guy."

He's not Mark.

"Mark's gone. He'd want me to be happy."

Wouldn't he? Maybe not. He'd been the jealous sort, asking way more questions about her relationships with the men in her kitchens than about the women as though looking for reasons to mistrust her.

Ancient history. Even when she and Mark had separated for those few months, she hadn't dated any of her coworkers. She hadn't been interested. She'd still been married to Mark, for starters. She'd loved him, faults and all.

She looked herself in the eye. "Granger is not Mark. They have nothing in common."

Did the woman in the mirror believe her? She wasn't sure she believed herself.

Also, maybe she'd stalled long enough. She didn't want to appear too eager, after all. Plus, she needed to report to the kitchen in an hour. She was looking forward to Tuesday and having a quiet table — maybe candlelit or fireside — to get to know each other over delectable entrées.

Also, Julia was curious.

Pam would have to play that part by ear. It wasn't like she was going to lie about her interest in the inn's guest.

When she stepped out onto the main floor Granger stood with his back to the elevator, hands behind his back, as he gazed out the wide bow window. Tall, strong, and true to his military bearing.

Julia turned the low music up a notch and waggled her eyebrows from behind the reception desk. Her eyes sparkled with glee. Or maybe mischief.

Pam shook her head at her friend then took a few seconds to appreciate Granger's fine figure... and to shove Mark the rest of the way out of her head before strolling closer. "Hi. Julia said you wanted to see me?"

He turned on his heel and looked her up and down, a small smile plying at the corners of his mouth. "You look very nice today, Pam."

"Um, thank you. You do, too, but I doubt that's why you wanted to talk to me." She smiled to remove the sting. Wow, she needed to learn a bit more tact.

"No." He sighed. "It's true, but it's not the news I need to share. That's about Tuesday."

Pam's eyebrows tilted upward as her stomach plummeted. "Oh?"

"You know my reason for being in Jewel Lake is to get to know my daughter and my grandchildren. I'll be honest. It's been hard going with Melissa. She didn't know she wasn't the daughter of her mother's husband until she was a teenager, then Denise never painted me in the best light. Melissa's been reluctant to give me much room in her life." Granger rubbed a hand across his jaw.

This had to be going somewhere, but where? Pam was at a loss, but she could feel her walls coming up, just the same.

"She's a pharmacist assistant at the drugstore downtown, and she's being sent to a conference in Salt Lake in place of her boss, who's down with the flu."

Glimmers of understanding poked through the fog.

"She leaves late this afternoon and returns Wednesday… and she asked me to stay at her house with the children."

"Ahhh. I understand." What Pam didn't get was why the disappointment was so keen, so deep. She barely knew this man, but she'd been so primed to spend one-on-one time with him and learn more. She could understand Melissa's reluctance, but this sounded like a great breakthrough for Granger's relationship with his daughter's family. "You'll be busy."

"Yeah." He ran a hand through his short hair, causing a few tufts to stick at strange angles.

Pam willed herself not to reach up and smooth those strands back into place. When had he lost the military buzz cut? Soldier Granger must have cut quite a sight in uniform.

"And even if I made an attempt to make something work for Tuesday, it's Sidney's figure skating practice, so I'm stuck."

Granger bit his lip and studied Pam's face. "I really hate to ask you for a rain-check. That's no way to begin… whatever this is."

"I understand." She gulped. "Family comes first."

"Thanks." His smile might be fleeting, but softness had replaced the wariness in his eyes. "One week later?"

"Sure. I'm not going anywhere. At least, not for a couple of more months." Maybe.

Granger lowered his voice. "I did realize something this afternoon, though." His gaze flicked past her then refocused.

She tipped her head toward his. "Oh?"

"I need your phone number. Julia was — is — all kinds of curious. I wasn't sure if you'd told her anything."

"Is she watching us now?" Pam resisted the urge to check for herself.

"She's pretending not to, if I don't miss my guess."

"Has she overheard?"

"I don't think so. We've kept our voices down, and the music probably covered our conversation."

"She's going to ask me. I know it."

"What will you tell her?"

"What do you suggest?"

His eyes gleamed, and that hint of a smile grew. "There's always the truth."

"Truth is good. I'm just not sure I want five friends in my business."

"It must be nice to have five friends who care so much about you."

Pam blinked. He was absolutely right. She might have kept herself aloof over the years — living far from the others had helped with that — but any one of all of these women would have come running anytime she asked. They'd all come to Mark's funeral. She'd flown here to Montana when George passed away.

On neither of those occasions had anyone known what to say to each other, but they'd come. And their presence had made the difference.

She'd never been alone. Not completely. Had she ever truly thanked her friends for their staunch support?

Now she pulled her phone from her pocket and opened it before handing it to Granger with a smile. "You're right. We need each other's contact info."

Granger should have asked for Pam's number Friday night. Why hadn't he? Maybe he'd thought she was a talk-only kind of person, which he definitely was not. Texting was so much more his style that he nearly always had his ringer turned off, but many of his age-mates complained about texting. One of his fellow instructors at the military college refused to carry anything but a dumb phone.

Granger had always figured it had more to do with comfort with technology than what decade someone was born. He'd had to keep up with the times whether he wanted to or not. Mostly, he'd wanted to.

Now, he scanned the brief conversation from Sunday evening.

Granger: *Just checking in. How were things in the kitchen tonight?*

Pam: *Rave reviews, I hear. [smiley face emoji]*

Granger: *Good to hear! Friday was certainly a feast.*

Pam: *The menu was more ordinary tonight.*

Yeah, he bet.

Granger: *Well, I don't want to keep you up.*

Not like he had Friday… though he'd certainly be willing to repeat that any time she was willing. If it became a habit, he might need to readjust his workout time. Six had come mighty early the next day.

Pam: *I'll be awake for a while yet. It takes time to come down off the rush.*

So, they'd chatted a bit longer. The kids had been in bed,

Sidney protesting all the way. Hey, her grandfather didn't make the rules, just tried to enforce what her mother had laid out.

Now, it was mid-morning on Monday, and Granger had such a brilliant idea that he nearly smacked his head. Duh! The kids were in school until 3:00. That meant he had free time... and Pam might, too.

Granger: *What are you up to this morning? For lunch? I'm free until 3!*

Pam: *Just a sec.*

He waited, drumming his fingers against Melissa's kitchen table. Then he waited some more. It must have been ten minutes before his phone chimed again. Okay, maybe only three.

Pam: *Sorry about that. I was just in a meeting with Julia about this week's menu. Done now.*

Granger: *On your day off?*

Pam: *It doesn't matter. But you should know she asked about you.*

His chest warmed.

Granger: *Oh? What did you tell her?*

Pam: *...*

Granger: *That's not much of an answer! LOL*

Pam: *Okay, fine. I told her you seemed like a nice guy and that you'd asked me out.*

Granger: *And...*

Pam: *[innocent whistling emoji]*

He couldn't help it. He laughed out loud. Good thing there was no one in this little house to see or hear.

Granger: *So... how about lunch?*

Pam: *Is there someplace besides the Golden Grill?*

Granger: *You didn't like the food there?*

Pam: *It was more the atmosphere. Also, that woman is far too nosy. If we went there for lunch, we'd be engaged by dinner and married by sundown.*

He blinked. Then laughed again.

Granger: *That doesn't sound terrible. I'm up for it if you are.*

Wait, what? Had he just sort of offhandedly proposed to a

woman he barely knew? On the other hand, if she didn't have a sense of humor, now was the best time to find out. She certainly hadn't seemed like she had a funny bone the first time they'd crossed paths in that establishment.

Pam: *Not today, thanks.*

Hopefully, that was humor.

Granger: *I'll try not to feel too harshly rejected. There's the Rendezvous Restaurant at the hotel. We could try that instead.*

Pam: *Sounds good. I can meet you there at noon. I have a few errands to run downtown this afternoon anyway.*

So much for picking her up like a proper date. Were the conventions the same for people in their fifties as when he'd been 19 and taken Denise out the first time? He'd waited on the doorstep with his hat in his hand.

He didn't even wear hats anymore, unless knitted beanies in winter counted.

Granger: *Perfect. I'll see you then.*

That gave him just over an hour for his quiet time. His schedule was out of whack, since he couldn't very well leave the house until the kids were ready for school. He'd dropped them off on his way to the gym.

He hadn't really spent a lot of time since his meeting with Pastor Marshall on Thursday to contemplate the man's request. Did Granger have the skill set to make an event happen, especially in a town where he didn't know many people? No, he did not.

But God specialized in the impossible. Granger had seen that time and time again over the years, so that wasn't really one of the considerations. If God wanted him to do this, his liabilities wouldn't be an issue.

The bigger question was whether this was God's calling on Granger Durand... or not.

He opened his Bible to his current reading plan. He might be a texting kind of man, but he preferred holding his physical Bible with its weathered leather cover and his scribbled notes in the margins to reading from an app.

Isaiah 43 was on tap today. It wasn't that long, only 28 verses. He began reading.

But now, O Jacob, listen to the Lord who created you… Do not be afraid, for I have ransomed you.

Okay. Maybe God could speak to Granger through an obscure passage from the Old Testament. He'd claimed verse five before:

Do not be afraid, for I am with you. I will gather you and your children from east and west.

Granger only had one child, but he'd trusted God to gather her… and God had come through, answering that request.

In today's chapter, God recounted some of His acts of deliverance for Israel, but the tone changed at verse 18.

But forget all that — it is nothing compared to what I am going to do. For I am about to do something new. See, I have already begun! Do you not see it? I will make a pathway through the wilderness. I will create rivers in the dry wasteland.

Granger read the chapter again. Was this about Pastor Marshall's request? Or was it about Pam? Was it about both? Neither?

He bowed his head. Discernment always started with prayer.

CHAPTER
Nine

P am stopped just inside the Rendezvous and glanced around, but the hostess appeared before she had a chance to locate Granger. Maybe he wasn't here yet.

"Table for one?"

Pam smiled. "Not today. I'm meeting a friend."

"The gentleman by the window?"

Granger lifted his hand. Ah, there he was.

"Yes, thank you." Pam followed the woman to the high-backed booth, unzipping her jacket.

Granger rose and lifted her jacket from her shoulders as she shed it.

There weren't any hooks, so she took it from him with murmured gratitude and laid it on the bench.

"Thanks for joining me." He waited until she sat before resuming his seat.

Be still her heart. "My pleasure."

"May I get you something for starters? Water? Coffee?" The woman laid two menus on the table.

Pam had nearly forgotten the hostess's presence. "Both, please."

"Same." Granger nodded.

Pam glanced at Granger. He was studying her, which felt a little disconcerting. The menu seemed safer. "What's good here?"

"I'm not sure. I think we have to guess. I did check to see if they had Reubens on the menu, and it appears they do."

She blinked. He remembered what she'd ordered that day at the Golden Grill? All she'd seen in him was an indulgent grandfather of two reckless, rude children. Until she realized he'd paid for her lunch.

"I'm not sure I'm up for a Reuben today." She scanned the menu. "Perhaps the pear pecan salad."

"A salad?" He frowned slightly.

"There's grilled chicken breast with it."

"Do you mind if I have a burger?"

Why should she? She angled her head quizzically.

"I'm sure it's not up to your standards."

"I've enjoyed many a non-gourmet burger."

He blinked and met her gaze. "You have?"

"I'm not a food snob. I enjoy experimenting with interesting ingredients, especially local, in-season produce. But food is so much more, and sensory delight comes in many forms. Sometimes it is in simple comfort."

Granger closed his menu. "A burger it is."

"I..." Pam hesitated. Was this thing too new to speak her mind? Not if he were concerned about offending her with his meal choices. "I don't want you ever to order a certain way to gain my approval." She trailed her gaze boldly across the part of his body visible above the table. "You've obviously taken good care of yourself over the years, so your habits can't be that deplorable."

Granger's eyebrows bobbed. "You like what you see?"

Her face flushed. "If I didn't, I wouldn't have agreed to one date, let alone two."

"We've been out twice?" Amusement twinkled in his blue eyes.

"Not yet, but you've asked me twice."

"True, that. For what it's worth — and I hope it's worth quite a bit — I like what I see, too."

"Ready to order?" A server moved their beverages from a tray to the table.

Granger ordered for them both, which gave Pam a moment to regain her equilibrium. Was that even possible? The compliment had been understated, but the warm approval in his eyes spoke just as loudly as his words. She hadn't felt this off kilter since the early days with Mark.

The giddiness felt decidedly delicious.

Granger leaned back and stretched one arm across the top of the bench. "Tell me everything there is to know about Pamela Whorley."

"In three minutes or less?"

"Sure."

Those crinkles around his eyes when he smiled begged to be smoothed. Good thing she couldn't reach from here. But she sat on her hands, anyway, in case they betrayed her. "The reality will take less than that. I'm fairly boring. Work, eat, sleep."

"What do you do for hobbies?"

"Does perusing foodie magazines count?"

He snorted a laugh. "I don't think so."

"Then I don't have hobbies. I read a bit." Wow, she was dull.

"No knitting or crocheting?"

"Seriously, Granger? My grandmother was a knitter. I'm not old enough."

"My daughter knits."

"In that case, maybe I'm too old. I've heard it's had a resurgence in the younger generation, but I've never been tempted to pick it up again since I made a lopsided scarf when I was ten."

"Were you close to your grandmother?"

Pam blinked. How had he gotten to the heart of her so quickly? "She passed away that year. I have a few fond memories of her watching my sister and me after school. She lived next door."

"Ah, you have a sister! Older or younger?"

"Older. And I see what you're doing here." She traced her finger through the condensation on the side of her water glass.

Granger grinned. "Oh? What's that?"

"Making me remember."

"Do you not want to?" The smile diminished some.

"I don't know. There's so much pain mixed in with the good bits that it's easier not to sort through them. My grandmother died of a heart attack when she wasn't much older than I am now. My sister got into drugs. My parents divorced after she ran away as a teen. Later, we heard she died of an overdose. A friend talked me into going to Gilead Bible College with her, but then she got pregnant and bailed out after one semester. If it hadn't been for Wendy, Julia, and the others, I'm not sure what I'd have done, but the sisterhood was already forming."

"When did you meet Mark?"

Pam closed her eyes and exhaled long and slow. "He was an accountant who used to come into the restaurant where I worked. This whole group from his office came for lunch every day."

The aroma of grilled onions, meat, and cheese assaulted her nostrils, and she opened her eyes to see the server setting their plates down. She took a shaky breath as she looked at her salad. It looked fine — or, at least, okay — but maybe she wasn't hungry anymore. Dives into her deep pool of memories seemed to do that. She nudged her plate away slightly.

Granger's eyebrows twitched as he met her gaze.

This man missed nothing. Military training might tend to have that effect. Did Pam want to be analyzed? Because it felt safer to stay clammed up. Or to run. She shifted on her seat, and her fingers clenched her jacket lying beside her.

She couldn't do that to Granger. It wasn't his fault that her life was a bubbling inferno she barely managed to keep lidded. Once he figured that out, he wouldn't want to be dragged into it. So, maybe it was best he saw the truth now, before either of them was in too deep.

"I was a terrible wife and mother," she blurted. "I worked too much. Expected too much of the kids, of Mark, of everyone. I'm not a nice person, Granger. I'm really not. You shouldn't bother with me."

"Maybe I want to. Maybe I see value in you."

Pam managed a crooked smile. "I'm a mess."

"You're a woman God made and whom God loves. A loyal friend. A woman who can do anything she sets her mind to, who's afraid of nothing."

"I'm afraid of a lot of things." She stared at the neatly sliced grilled chicken.

"You drove across the country by yourself at a friend's request. That's brave right there."

"It wasn't, not really. Nothing was keeping me in Charleston." She'd kept everyone at arm's length after Mark's death. No one needed to know the ugly mix of relief and regret that swirled through her mind. The sleepless nights. The anguish. Yes, for all these years.

Granger took a few bites of his burger while he prayed. He felt a deep connection to Pam — so deep it was terrifying, honestly. But he didn't know what to do or say in response to her words. She was hurting, that much was plain.

He knew emotional pain, too. Like Pam, he'd tried to shovel enough work on top to smother it, but it had refused to be extinguished until he'd exposed his wound to God's mercy. He still bore scars, but the rawness was gone.

Pam carried hers still. She hadn't said how many years it had been since the accident that took her family, but it had to be at least ten years, maybe longer, if her kids had been the same age as Sidney and Oliver.

That was a long time to bear this burden alone, but how could he help her? Was it his job to do so? All he knew for certain was that godly friends prayed for each other. He could commit to that, at least.

Granger sipped his coffee. She picked up her fork and took a bite of salad. Good sign.

"You've been to Creekside Fellowship a couple of times now. What do you think? I'm sure it's a lot different than the big city church you probably attended in South Carolina."

"Very different."

Was it his imagination, or did she relax slightly at the change of topic?

"I went to a mega-church," she offered.

"It's easy to disappear in one of those." He'd done it himself, for a time.

"Sometimes that's the point. I felt like I could stay connected to my faith without the mess of the people around me intruding, you know?"

"God's church is made of humans. Like Pigpen in the Charlie Brown cartoons, we carry the mess with us wherever we go. We might bathe and comb our hair and put on clean clothes once in a while, but our true selves come out again shortly."

Her chuckle was mirthless. "You're painting a bleak picture of the church."

"Prove me wrong." He ate a couple of fries.

"I can't."

"The church is made up of sinners saved by grace, on the road together, trying to follow Jesus's teachings."

"Shouldn't I — we — have it all together by now? Inside, I don't feel any more mature than when I was 25."

At 25, Granger had been in the thick of things in Afghanistan. He could only hope he'd matured since those days, but she was right. He was still the same guy, deep inside, just with a bum knee and gray hair.

He leaned against the bench back. "I remember being 12 or 13 and thinking guys who were 18 were unbelievably mature."

Pam laughed.

"When I was 18, guys who were 30 seemed so far over the hill that I couldn't even see that far."

"True."

He was just getting warmed up. "At 40, men old enough to retire seemed decrepit with one foot in the grave. And here I am, pushing 60, and now I'm eyeing 80-year-olds with a similar thought."

"Maybe when you're 75, you'll still feel young and hip."

"I guess we'll see when we get there." He chuckled, thankful he'd distracted her a little. And suddenly, the next 30-plus years looked more like possibilities than like inevitable decline. Was that Pam's doing? He might have perked up some being included in Melissa's life, in Sidney's and Oliver's lives, but the door to a vibrant future had opened wider since he'd met Pam.

She might not be ready to hear that yet, though. Military training had taught him to gather intel and make a judgment call in seconds flat. There might not be time for a long perusal.

Things were different now. Life and death rarely balanced on an impulse decision, though it could. He had time to take things slow... but not too slow. He wasn't a young cock on the walk anymore. But neither was he ancient, that stupid knee notwithstanding.

"Anyway, one of the things I like about a small-town church is that the needs are more apparent. There isn't always a huge budget to throw at a perceived need. Sometimes a person looks around for the person who should be in charge of whatever, then realizes they might be the most qualified person in the room. That can be exhilarating as well as panic-inducing."

Pam met his gaze, one eyebrow lifting. "I'm not sure what you're trying to say here."

A woman who spoke directly. He liked that.

"I've got more time on my hands than I know what to do with, so I asked Pastor Marshall what I could do to help. I was envisioning something like raking the leaves in that park beside the church. Or maybe a small repair here or there. Painting a Sunday school room."

A small smile toyed with her mouth. "I take it he had something else in mind? Let me guess. Drumming?"

Granger chuckled. "No, that wasn't his doing. He asked me to plan a Thanksgiving outreach for folks in the community who are in need. I kind of think he got the wrong man. I might have planned a military mission or two, but I don't even know where to start with this one." He gave her his best puppy-dog eyes. "Any advice? He said there were plenty of people who would pitch in if told what to do, but that's not much help at this point."

"A Thanksgiving outreach?"

"With a dinner and a program, I think? He mentioned I'd make a great Santa."

Pam eyed him. "With a pillow or two."

"A svelte Santa isn't a thing?"

She snickered.

And that was the best sound he'd heard in a long time.

CHAPTER

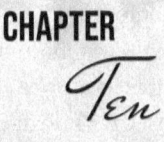

Ten

"M onte Newman seems to be hanging around here quite a bit." Pam eyed Julia. Maybe her tentative relationship with Granger gave her bravery in gently poking at her friend. "Anything I should know?"

Julia waved a hand. "Nothing at all." Although was that a slight flush creeping up her neck?

"I should hire the man to bake pies for our restaurant. He seems talented... and like he has time on his hands."

"Aren't his desserts great? He needs to stop before I pack on another 20 pounds."

"You still miss George..." Pam left that comment open-ended.

Julia's eyes misted over. "This inn was his dream. Mine, too, but it was he who worked hard to bring it to fruition. Did you know that George and Monte were friends from way back?"

Pam nodded. "You've mentioned that. From early days at their jobs in Seattle."

"Everywhere I look at Maranatha, I see George's touch. He worked with the architect to design this whole place. I've changed nothing. It was all in his plans."

"Did he design the 14 Christmas trees you're planning, too?"

"Oh, you!" Julia gave Pam a playful slap on the arm. "George knew how much I loved all things Christmas. There's just so much hope in the Advent season, you know? So much to be thankful for, even though I miss him dearly."

"That memo must have skipped me."

"The one for gratitude and hope?"

"Yeah. That one." Though Pam had glimpsed glimmers of both now that she'd cracked the door open.

"I know you miss Mark and the children."

The children who would be in their 20s and might even have made Pam a grandmother by now. But they were frozen to the age they'd been that fateful day. "It was doubly hard because of the kids. Courtney had been giving me lip about spending the weekend with Mark's parents. She figured she should be allowed to stay with a friend. We had a big argument before they left."

"Twelve-year-olds." Julia's smile was lopsided.

"Right? But I wish I hadn't been so harsh. And Mark…" Pam tightened her lips.

"Mark what, Pammy?"

Maybe she'd carried this by herself long enough. Would uttering the words remove their power? At least some of it? "Things were hard with Mark."

"I figured as much."

Pam looked at her friend through narrowed eyes. "You what?"

"Do you remember how I couldn't stop gushing about George in our group calls and text chats?"

"Of course, I remember." Pam rolled her eyes. "You were so sappy it was nearly sickening. Like honeymooners."

"George made me feel like a new bride every day. It was hard not to prattle about him, but we rarely heard Mark's name."

"There wasn't much to talk about. Let's say we weren't starry-eyed newlyweds, and leave it at that, shall we?"

"Maybe you need to talk about Mark now."

"Probably not. He's been gone a dozen years. That life is over."

"I don't want to push you…"

"Then don't." Pam managed a smile at her friend. "There's no need to dredge up ancient history. I'm okay."

"Because of Granger?"

Well, maybe, but also time. "I'm… cautiously optimistic. Granger seems really nice and, for some reason I don't understand, he likes me."

"I'm happy for you." Julia squeezed Pam tightly. "Also, what's not to like?"

"You know. I'm not that likable." Oof. She could hear Wendy's voice in her own words.

"Says who?" Julia giggled. "I think you're an amazing person, and I'm happy to call you my friend. And I'm delighted you accepted my call to come to Montana. Hasn't it been amazing to be all together again?"

"You do know that Audrey snipes at Wendy and that Chris avoids the rest of us, right? And that Laura is hiding a world of trouble behind that bounciness?"

"I'm praying for each of you. This is such a terrific opportunity for us all to move forward as a friend group. As a team."

"Are you always this optimistic?" But Pam knew the answer. That definitely was who Julia had always been. She'd been the glue that held them together in college and beyond. The light they'd all been attracted to.

"No," Julia said softly. "It was dark when George died. He wasn't supposed to, you know. I was going to plan his hundredth birthday way off in the future."

Pam got it. Mark wasn't supposed to die, either. They were going to give their marriage another go. They might have gone through all that counseling, exposed all their hurts, made all the necessary concessions… and quite possibly have failed, anyway. A healed relationship had been far from a foregone conclusion.

She reached for her friend impulsively. "I'm glad you kept going. I'm glad you invited us all. But we all brought our baggage, you know."

"I know. We can lay it at the foot of the cross together."

It was hard to hate someone so uplifting, who always pointed everyone to Jesus. But it was also annoying not to be allowed to wallow. Honestly, though, did Pam want to keep floundering? Wasn't a dozen years enough? She'd met someone new, which she had not planned on or even daydreamed about. She'd figured she'd remain alone until her dying day. Then her friends would gather around at her funeral and lament how hard her life had been, how bravely she'd faced those long, lonely decades.

Or... she could choose to live again. Life and love looked amazingly attractive right now, but surely Granger had a dark side, too. He couldn't possibly be as perfect as he seemed. This time, she'd figure it out before marriage, before she hitched her future to a fizzling star.

"Listen, I was on my way out. Monte's sister phoned and asked me if I could pick Maggie up from skating practice. Sheryl has a meeting at work she can't get out of, and her husband is working. Monte was off to Missoula to get the tires changed on his truck before Sheryl realized she needed help covering for her granddaughter. Want to come with me?"

"Sure. But isn't Sheryl Maggie's grandmother? Where are the girl's parents?"

"Kyle is on a job in Seeley Lake. And there's no mother in the picture." Julia chuckled, shaking her head. "You're lucky you're not anywhere near Kyle's age, because Maggie keeps begging for a mom. Kyle is at his wit's end because Maggie often asks random women if they'll date her dad and marry him."

"Sounds... adorable."

"Only Maggie thinks so." Julia glanced at the clock. "I need to scoot to get her now, though. Someone will pick her up from here later."

"I have nothing better to do." Pam had thought she'd be getting ready for a date with Granger about now, but he'd canceled due to his grandkids. Wait... hadn't he said his granddaughter skated on Tuesday afternoons? Maybe she'd run into him at the arena! Suddenly what was left of her day off seemed a whole lot brighter.

"This is so boring." Oliver slumped on the hard, wooden bleachers beside Granger. "When will it be over?"

"Your sister still has ten minutes left to skate. Then she has to change before we can go home."

"That's like forever."

"Quit whining, kid." Even if Melissa put up with that nonsense out of Oliver, that didn't mean Granger had to. "Remember we're getting takeout on our way home."

"It's not your home."

"You're right, but I'm staying at *your* house one more night, so it's my home for now." He'd tried so hard to make inroads with the kids, but they missed their mom, and a grandfather apparently was a poor substitute. Was he supposed to spoil them rotten? He'd been trying, but too many years of trying to shape up 18-year-old cadets who'd lived with few rules before entering boot camp had soured him from adding to the nation's problem.

"Who's that?" Oliver pointed toward the exit doors.

Granger pushed the boy's hand down even as he looked over. Then he did a double-take. What were Pam and Julia doing here? He waved.

They waved back and made their way toward him.

"That's Mrs. Cox who runs Maranatha Inn and Mrs. Whorley, who is the chef there."

The boy's brows furrowed, but before Granger could explain further — though what was there to say? — the women had arrived on the bench below them.

"Hi!" Julia beamed. "You're Oliver, right?"

"Yeah?"

Granger nudged him.

The boy sighed and held out his hand. "I'm Oliver Everett. Pleased-to-meet-you."

Sounded like one word, but at least he'd been polite.

Julia shook it. "I'm Mrs. Cox."

"That's what Gramps said. Why are you here?"

"See that girl in the purple leggings and sweatshirt?"

Oliver scanned the rink. "Yeah?"

"That's my friend's granddaughter, Maggie Johannesson. Do you know her?"

"Yeah, my sister doesn't like her much."

"Oh, that's too bad. Your sister is missing out on a potential great friend. Maggie is a good kid, but she doesn't have a terrific brother like you."

Granger caught Pam's smirk from beyond Julia. Glad she thought it was funny about Sidney. But then again, Pam had met Sidney at her worst and still liked Granger, so he could let it go. "Hey, nice to see you here. Surprising, but nice."

She glanced toward Julia, who was still chatting with Oliver, then came around to sit on Granger's other side. "She's here to pick up Maggie. I guess the other adults in her life couldn't make it."

Granger's eyebrows tipped up of their own accord. "And yet there's nothing between Julia and Monte."

"I know, right?" Pam sobered. "In some ways, she's moved forward from George, but in other ways, she's not ready to let go of him. They had an exemplary marriage."

"Must have been nice." Granger watched Pam from the corner of his eye.

"Must've been." She stared straight ahead, biting her lip.

He held back his sigh. What made him think he could do a better job now? Age was on his side. Hopefully, maturity was, too. Faith was certainly a much deeper foundation for him now than in his younger years.

But it took two, and was Pam as invested as he was?

He coughed lightly to cover the scoff bubbling up his throat. He barely knew the woman beside him. How could he have fallen so hard, so quickly, that he was actually contemplating something permanent between them?

"You okay?" Pam eyed him.

"I'm fine. Sorry about that."

"How's Melissa's conference going?"

"Okay, I think, from what she's said. She'll be back tomorrow evening in time to tuck the kids in."

"How has it been for you?"

Granger glanced at his grandson, who gestured as though he were telling an animated story. Bless Julia for connecting with the boy. "It's been okay. Sidney's given me some sass, but she's coming around. Same with Ollie, honestly, though not as much. They figure I'm too strict."

"Are you?" Pam smirked.

"I don't know. I've never raised kids. I have no idea what I'm doing."

Her smile flattened.

If he could have kicked himself in the rear, he would have. "I'm sorry. I wasn't trying to remind you."

"I know. It's not your fault. Everything, everywhere, is a reminder. If they think you're too strict, then I guess you're in good company. At least, if my company is good. Courtney always said I'd never let her have any fun with her friends."

Granger leaned slightly to press his shoulder against Pam's. He didn't dare take her hand in present company. "Let me guess. '*Dad* would let me.'"

"How'd you guess? And I think Mark allowed a lot when the kids stayed with him on weekends for those few months we were separated."

"Melissa's kids say that, too, except they don't see their father. Chad went south to work on the oil rigs in the Gulf and they only see him a couple of times a year. Even though he essentially abandoned them, they still figure it would be better with him around."

"Kids never know how good they've got it. I'm sure Sidney and Oliver appreciate you more than you think."

The arena buzzer sounded, and the dozen tween girls on the ice skated toward the dressing room. Maggie Johannesson waved at Julia and blew her kisses. Sidney didn't even glance their way.

Granger could only hope Sidney was thankful for her grandfather. He was thankful for her. Thankful for another chance with Melissa and the children. He'd offered Denise his sincere apology for not working harder to uphold their marriage way back when, but it was too little and much too late. She'd been married to Grant for 35 years and considered Granger a youthful indiscretion.

Which was fair. An indiscretion who hadn't understood the gravity of the vows he was making. Hadn't prioritized them.

Water under the bridge. There was nothing he could do for Denise. Only for Melissa, Sidney, and Oliver.

But if he could also help wipe the sorrow from Pam's face and heart, he'd consider that a win.

P ajama party!" Laura struck a cheerleading pose and twirled imaginary pompoms. "We needed some girl time before Pammy comes home with a diamond."

Pam nearly choked on her iced tea. "Who said anything about getting married again?"

"You have a date with a hot veteran tomorrow. Why are you going out with him if you're not looking at the future?"

A question Pam had asked herself dozens of times. "Because he's a nice guy?"

"So are we." Laura dropped into a chair and thumbed to Audrey on one side of her and Chris on the other. "You don't need to leave Maranatha to find nice people."

Was marriage Granger's endgame? Probably not. He knew Pam was here temporarily. As far as she knew, he wasn't fully committed to staying in Jewel Lake, either. They were just friends, passing the time in pleasant company.

Right? But if she couldn't convince herself, how would she ever convince her friends?

"It's okay, Pam. If you're ready to remarry, don't let anyone else's opinions hold you back." Wendy stared Laura down across the round table in the staff lounge.

"I'm just teasing her. No need to get all defensive." Laura wrinkled her nose at Wendy.

"Anyone in this room is free to date and marry if they wish." Audrey's nose seemed a little higher in the air than necessary.

Maybe Pam shouldn't read too much into that.

"First we have to find a man who'll give us a second look." Audrey glanced at Wendy.

Ugh.

"And Pammy has dibsed the only currently available one," Laura went on. "Except there's our neighbor, Monte."

"Who only has eyes for Julia," Pam interrupted. "So, I think he's off the table for anyone else."

"Julia says she's not interested." Laura raised her eyebrows at Julia.

"It takes two," Chris put in. "But Monte is definitely interested in Julia."

"He is not!" Julia threw up both hands. "He and Karen were friends of George's and mine for decades. The men loved fishing and hiking together. He's being a good neighbor. That's it. There's no endgame, as you put it."

"All I'm saying is there's a shortage of available men around here." Laura tossed her hair back. "That's the one big downside to joining your Maranatha project, Julia."

"I suppose you had a date every week in Maine?" Pam couldn't hold back the barbed question.

"If I wanted one, yes."

"It only takes one man. The right man." Julia looked between them. "And you girls are reminding me of college, when we were all on the hunt for our forever loves."

"Forever love." Audrey rolled her eyes. "It turns out that the male species is fickle. You're the lucky one, Chris. Never had your heart broken."

"Thanks. I think."

Pam studied Chris for a few seconds. Was that true? Had Chris never even been in love? She'd been optimistic in college, but men didn't seem to see her as desirable. She'd never been overly feminine, and maybe that had been a turnoff for some. But Chris couldn't help who she was. Why should she pretend to care about makeup and fashion and flirting when she really didn't? She'd found work as an arborist in a man's world. As far as Pam knew, Chris had never been in a serious relationship. If she'd even dated over the years, she'd kept it to herself.

Was it better to have loved and lost than never to have loved at all?

Hmm. Pam had two minds about that. At least their other friends had children to comfort them as solo adults. Sometimes Pam wished she'd held out like Chris did. Her memories rammed any hopes of the future against an unforgiving brick wall.

Even with Granger. Maybe especially with Granger, because of those two grandkids who reminded Pam far too much of Courtney and Roderick.

No, he was one of the good guys. He truly was. She should consider staying in Montana long-term if things worked out.

"How's Michael doing without you at home?" Wendy asked Laura.

"Oh, just fine." Laura waved a hand. "Katie's mom has stepped in to watch Ruby part-time. It's my granddaughter I miss! Three is such a fun age. But Michael and Katie are good parents, and Katie's in her element running the Beachcomber. They don't need me."

Pam recalled Laura's confession of pregnancy just before their graduation from Gilead. Their friend group didn't even know for sure whom she'd been dating. Pam had her guesses, but Laura had refused to say who her baby's father was. After graduation, Laura had retreated to Maine where she'd birthed and raised Michael on her own until she'd married Gord. That union hadn't lasted long, though.

Somehow, Laura had managed the purchase of a beachside B&B when she'd first moved home. Maybe her parents had financed it. The details weren't clear. Either way, she'd had a home and a business wrapped up in one.

"Well, too bad my little brother is too young for any of you." Audrey examined her fingernails. "Did I mention he's planning an extended visit next fall? I'll talk to you about reserving a room for him, Julia, but it's months away yet."

"Roman?" Wendy asked. "What's he been up to, anyway?"

Audrey looked around the table before focusing on Wendy. "He travels all the time for the import business our father and uncle started. Roman is in… I'm not sure where he is right now. Somewhere in Asia? No, that was last spring. I forgot you'd remember him."

Wendy laughed. "Of course, I do. He was such a cute little guy, following us around all the time."

"I hated babysitting him. Parents should *not* space their only children nine years apart. That's just rude to the older child. But I guess he's turned out okay, all things considered."

"I'm sure we can book a long-stay room for him." Julia leaned over the table. "Let me reserve something when I'm at the front desk one of these days. We've had an inquiry from an author, as well, who's looking for an inspiring view for a few months. I'd been hoping to attract some longer-term guests, so this is perfect."

"The view is definitely inspiring," Pam put in. "Now, were we going to play Hand and Foot, or were we going to gab all night? If we're playing three teams, I'm with Chris. Julia and Laura are across from each other, and so are Audrey and Wendy. Hopefully no one needs to trade places."

She laughed, but could Audrey and Wendy play nicely together? It was just a game, after all.

"Sure, we're good." Audrey nodded at Wendy across the table. "Right?"

"Of course. I'll shuffle."

Granger liked his new habit, and he loved that Pam seemed to enjoy it, too. Every night this week he'd waited by the fireplace in the lobby until the kitchen lights dimmed and Pam's shift was over. The inn was locked down, and Laura, who'd been at the front desk tonight, was off duty unless someone pressed the buzzer outside.

Granger had fixed two cups of hot chocolate from the beverage station beside the elevators. No doubt, Pam's creation would be far tastier than these packets, but it was the company that counted, at least for him.

Pam came toward him on her softly padded shoes, and he stood to greet her with a hug. Honestly? The hug was the best part of waiting up for her. "Hey. How was work tonight?"

"Good." She sighed against his chest as her arms closed around his back. "Busy, but good. That's the most plates we've fixed since opening night."

"Word's getting out."

She shifted against him, and he dropped his arms. "That's the hope."

"And it's working." He indicated the coffee table with two steaming mugs. "I brought you a hot chocolate."

"Oh, thank you. That sounds perfect." She sank onto the love seat and reached for one of the mugs. "Smells good."

"Mmm." Granger took a sip of his. "I had another meeting with Pastor Marshall this afternoon."

"Oh? About that event he wants you to plan?"

"Yeah. I asked what his Plan B was, and he pointed at me, laughed, and said he didn't have one."

"Way to put on pressure."

"True, but I also haven't been able to get it out of my mind. Does that mean God wants me to do it?"

Pam looked at him across the top of her mug, her eyebrows peaking.

"I'm not asking you to decide that for me." He chuckled and set his mug back on the coffee table. "I was thinking about Wendy."

"Oh?"

Was Pam's voice a little frostier? "She knows how to do events, right? I'm floundering a bit here. I don't even know what I don't know."

"I'm sure you could search online."

"I keep forgetting about that option. But do you think she'd mind if I picked her brain? Or does she not have the skill set?"

"She probably does. She ran all kinds of fundraisers for her homeschool co-op and for her husband's business. She'd probably be happy to help."

"You're not happy I want to ask."

Her nose scrunched and then she laughed. "Is it silly I got a little jealous right there?"

Granger slid one arm around Pam's shoulder and pulled her closer. "I'm not interested in Wendy. I'm interested in you."

"Why not her?" Pam's eyebrows tipped up.

He blinked. What kind of question was that? "Uh... I'd noticed you before I ever met her." He caressed Pam's shoulder. "I don't have eyes for anyone else. You're it."

What was he saying? It seemed his feelings were way ahead of Pam's, but that didn't mean she wasn't with the program. She had a full-time job and all her friends here, but she hadn't come to Montana to fall in love.

Neither had Granger. He'd even repelled the notion at first, but resistance had been futile. He'd slid from interest to like to maybe more in just a few weeks flat.

She looked up at him, her eyes searching his.

"Trust me..." He tugged her closer. "You're the one I want to be with."

"Okay." Her response was barely audible as she looked up at him.

Granger leaned in. Pam's face tilted to his. Her lips were slightly parted. Lips he longed to taste. Was he moving too quickly? His other hand lifted to tuck her hair behind her ear, to caress her cheek, to stroke her neck. "May I?" he whispered.

Her eyes drifted shut in reply.

He'd take that as a yes. This kiss would be gentle. Brief. Sweet. He touched his lips to hers, and the intensity of the longing that flashed through him caught him by surprise.

Pam's eyelids sprang open, her eyes wide, her mouth still open and kissable.

Looked like he wasn't the only one who might have expected the contact to feel more platonic. That had not been an innocent peck between friends. It was more.

And yet, not enough. He brushed his thumb across her cheek. Across her lips.

She inhaled sharply, and her eyes fluttered shut.

Granger feathered kisses over her eyelids, and her hands crept around his neck as though to hold him in place. Not to worry. He wasn't going anywhere. Not for a good while, anyway. For a few more seconds, his lips explored her face, as he reveled in the feel of her hands in his short hair and her ratcheting pulse. His was right there with hers, and the tension was delicious.

Not as delicious as a kiss, and he wasn't about to prolong his own agony, let alone hers. He settled his mouth over hers and kissed her like a man seeking enough oxygen to stay alive.

Because that's what it felt like. Even ten minutes ago, he hadn't known he was dying without her kisses. Now, he knew.

He sensed her pulling away, and forced his lips from hers, though he still couldn't get enough of the current humming between them. "Pam..."

"Wow." She touched his cheek. "I wasn't expecting that."

"I asked..."

Pam shook her head. "I meant, I wasn't expecting so many... sparks."

"You felt them, too?"

"So much. I didn't know..."

He cupped her face in his hands and rested his forehead against hers. "Didn't know what?"

"I didn't know it could be like this again."

"I didn't, either. Guess we're not too old." He couldn't help the grin.

"Seems so." Pam traced her finger down his jaw then peeked up at him. "Can we do that again?"

"Oh, my lady. I thought you'd never ask."

Yep, good thing he'd changed his workout time at the gym, because meshing his schedule to Pam's was worth every minute of staying up late.

CHAPTER
Twelve

H ere, have a cup of tea." Pam set a teacup in front of Wendy. Granger already had his, and so did she.

"Thank you." Wendy studied Granger across the round table in the dining room. "You wanted to talk to me?"

Pam tried not to cringe as Wendy ladled several heaping spoons of sugar into her cup. It wasn't any of her business. She knew that.

Wendy stirred her tea and looked at Granger again. "What's up?"

He glanced at Pam before turning back to Wendy. "I understand you're experienced at planning events."

Wendy clasped her hands together, and her eyes lit up. "Already? Wow, you two are sure moving quickly!"

What? No! Pam reared back.

Granger cleared his throat and shook his head. "A church outreach event, not anything more... ah... personal."

"Oh." Wendy's fair cheeks reddened in an instant. "Sorry. I jumped to conclusions. Okay. Let's start again. What do you have in mind?"

Granger outlined what the pastor had asked of him while Wendy nodded and asked questions.

Pam listened. He'd put a lot of thought into this already. It seemed he mostly needed confirmation that he was on the right path.

"So, we need to plan a program and a menu." Wendy nodded firmly. "Pam, what do you think would be the best way to divvy out food prep to individuals in the church while still creating a quality banquet?"

"Um, good question. I've never created a menu under these parameters. I'm assuming comfort food rather than haute cuisine."

"For sure. The dollars spent need to fill bellies and give a sense of well-being."

"Excellent food can do that, as well."

"No offense, but when someone needs comfort food, mac-and-cheese is on the menu, not caviar."

Pam bit her lip. Hard. Wendy was right, tough as it was to acknowledge. "You're asking for mac-and-cheese to be on the menu? It's Thanksgiving!"

"It's a traditional side dish for many, and we're inviting families, right? Families with small kids who might prefer something familiar. I don't mean making it out of a box. I'm sure you have a great recipe to dress it up a little."

Pam did not. She'd never placed it on the menu in any of her kitchens... but Wendy had a point.

"So, turkey." Pam thought hard. "We can get church women to roast however many are needed. We'll need an estimated number of attendees soon. Turkey, dressing, mashed potatoes, gravy, green bean casserole — I have this great Green Bean Amandine recipe—"

"Amandine means almonds?" Wendy interrupted. "We can't serve known allergens."

"Dairy is an allergen," Pam countered. "So are wheat and

eggs. We can't eliminate every possible trigger and still have a great meal for a crowd."

Wendy shook her head. "No nuts."

Pam raised both hands in self-defense. It wasn't every day someone ordered her what to serve or not serve, but this also wasn't the moment to argue. Wendy had been on the defensive since her arrival, and she was taking charge now. Pam loved her friend enough to allow her voice to be heard.

She'd study that green bean casserole recipe later and see if she could adapt it. "Besides those, you're suggesting mac-and-cheese. We need a spot of brightness both visually and gastronom-ically. Brussels sprouts are traditional."

"Ugh." Wendy wrinkled her nose. "Those must be an acquired taste."

Who was the chef here? And how could Pam counter Wendy's plebeian tastebuds? "Granger?" After all, he'd been sitting there quietly listening. This was his event, not hers or Wendy's.

"Peas."

"What?"

"They're green, and more people like them. They're also cheaper."

Whose side was he on, anyway? Guilt poked. The side of the disadvantaged families they were trying to serve.

Granger folded his hands over his spiral-bound notebook. "My grandkids wouldn't touch a Brussels sprout with a ten-foot pole, but they'll eat peas and carrots."

Courtney and Roderick had consumed them, but she'd refused to take no for an answer. No chef's offspring would dare to argue about their food. But Pam knew when she was outnumbered. "Also, a salad of some sort."

"Just a basic one with familiar dressings. Ranch and Italian should cover most preferences." Wendy raised her eyebrows as though daring Pam to argue.

Yeah, Pam wanted to fight for a bit more class. So much could be done to rev a salad's effect on diners' tastebuds. "Okay. Any thoughts on dessert?"

Wendy wiggled in her chair, and it creaked a little. She beamed. "Something pumpkin and something apple?"

"Those mini cheesecakes opening night were terrific," Granger said. "Are they too time consuming? I could give you a hand in the kitchen if you thought it would help."

"And then an apple slice. I have a great recipe." Wendy grimaced. "I'm sure you do, too."

Repeat after me: this is not all about me. This is for Wendy and the greater good.

"I'd love to take a look at your recipe."

Wendy brightened. "You would? Great!"

Pam glanced over the notes she'd taken. She hated to admit it, but this menu was something more easily divided between the church women than something she would have planned on her own. Her menus were generally meant to impress. This one... would not, but it did meet the need.

"Okay, a program. Not sure what to do with that." Granger tapped his pen against the table.

Pam eyed Wendy. "I wonder if Laura still sings."

Wendy's eyes lit up. "Oh, she had a fabulous voice, didn't she! We can ask her. She might need accompaniment, or maybe she can download a track to sing to."

"Special music would be good." Granger made a note. "And, I guess, a speaker. Anything for the kids? We're wanting a family friendly affair, and so far, all I can say is Sidney and Oliver would be bored."

"A skit? A puppet play?" Wendy mused.

Pam held up both hands. "Here's where I have no opinions."

Granger's eyes crinkled as he grinned at her. "I never thought I'd live to hear that."

"Me, neither." Wendy laughed. "Well, I've raised six kids, and they were rarely bored. Let me think on this a bit. I'm sure I can come up with something."

"Six?" Granger's eyes widened.

"Six." Wendy's eyes teared up even as she smiled. "Adriel, Silas, Theo, Ezra, Selah, and Faith, ranging in age from 27 to 16. I even have three grandchildren."

Granger's mouth opened and closed a few times before he managed a single word. "Congratulations."

"Six kids!" Granger had hardly been able to wait for Wendy to enter the elevator before he turned back to Pam.

"It's not that unusual." Although, not in Pam's immediate circle where all adults had their eyes on the corporate ladder.

"She looks so… normal."

Pam laughed. "She is. I haven't met her family often, but they seemed like decent humans the times I have. Amazing, considering their father."

"I'm not sure I want to know about him."

"Let's just say Dave deserves more than a swift kick where it hurts for how he treated her. Wendy was such a devoted wife and mother, and he was busy having affairs on the side. He finally left Wendy and married a girl not much older than his own firstborn daughter. He's a creep."

"Ugh." Granger grimaced. "Guys like that give men a bad name."

"You said it."

"It must be hard for her to be here so far from her family. Do you think she'll stay?"

"I don't know." Pam pursed her lips. "Julia only asked any of us for a three-month commitment. Chris, of course, is all in and has been for over a year. She loves running the Christmas tree farm and living in the old farmhouse — Julia stayed there with her while the inn was being built. But the rest of us? I don't know."

"I hope you are considering it."

Pam met his gaze. "I might be. I guess it depends."

It depended on him. On how their relationship went. Or didn't. But was she really open to staying indefinitely? Unlike Wendy, she had no real ties to her previous life. Unless... "Are your parents still alive?"

She looked down at her hands twisting the teacup on the table. "Dad's gone. Mom was in a care facility until she passed recently. She had dementia and rarely remembered who I was in the last few years."

"That must have been hard."

"You have no idea." She laughed mirthlessly. "Unless... maybe you do know."

"I don't, not personally. My parents have been gone for years. My sister and I were never close. I see her every two or three years. She lives in Texas."

"I have no sibling anymore."

Not since her sister died as a teen. "You really have been alone."

She closed her eyes. "Yes."

Granger didn't dare tell her she didn't need to be alone anymore. He'd be beside her as long as she let him. Yeah, a man pushing 60 needed to realize he might well die before a woman five years his junior but, potentially, they could still have many good years together.

It was too soon to talk about that. He'd come close enough to the heart of the issue, and she'd said she'd consider it. His job was to make the consideration easy, a no-brainer. That she would see him as a safe haven. *Her* safe haven.

"Is there anything else you need to discuss about the dinner for now?"

Did he? He blinked and looked down at his notebook. "I'm going to run this by Pastor Marshall before taking it farther. He or

Eli might have ideas to add to the program. Do you think we need much more?"

Pam shook her head. "You'll need an MC. You could ask Eli or you could do it yourself."

"Me?" He thumbed his chest. "You've got the wrong man."

"You said you'd taught at a military college. Surely, you're not afraid to stand in front of a microphone."

He mimicked her tone. "Surely, you jest."

"Maybe." She tilted her head. "But it still surprises me."

"I guess I'll see what Marshall says, but honestly? I'd like to enjoy the evening with Melissa, Sidney, and Oliver." He hesitated. "Would you care to join our table? I'd love to have you as my date."

"I…" She snapped her mouth closed.

Granger swallowed his disappointment that she didn't seem eager to meet his family. Those kids had really made a lousy first impression that wouldn't easily be overcome.

"I'll let you know, okay?" Her voice was softer.

"Sure. It's still a few weeks away. Plenty of time." Unless they decided to assign seating, but that wasn't today's problem. He glanced at the clock. "We've got over an hour before you need to start work. Would you like to go for a walk up the hill?"

"To the tree farm? That would be nice. I need to change my shoes, though."

Why did women insist on wearing uncomfortable footwear? "I'll run upstairs and put away my notebook and meet you back in the lobby in a few?"

"Run?" Her eyebrows rose.

"I can run! My knee isn't that bad." He ran on the treadmill nearly every day, after all. It was part of the regimen that kept him fit long after he'd retired from active duty.

"Me, I'm going to take the elevator to my room. And back." She grinned.

"See? You'll have it tied up. I'm simply being a gentleman to leave it at your beck and call."

"There's always the one at the other end of the building."

Granger waved a hand in dismissal. "It's too far out of my way. I can do the stairs faster."

Pam rose and pushed in her chair. "See you in five."

"I'll be here." He tucked the notebook in his chest pocket and reached for her hand, but she didn't take his. Okay, fine, she wasn't ready for that in public, not that anyone was around.

Other than Julia at the front desk as they passed by, but she was busily typing on her keyboard and didn't even glance up.

Pam pressed the elevator button and smiled at him.

He couldn't take her reluctance personally. Hopefully, she'd be willing to clasp hands as they walked. Maybe he could even steal a kiss or two along the way.

Whistling, he took the stairs two at a time.

Below, he heard Pam's laugh as the elevator doors opened.

It did his heart good.

CHAPTER

Thirteen

Mark always said she was too much. Or that she was a lot.

At first, it had seemed like a compliment. Pam had teased him that she was too much woman, and he needed to man up. After a few years, she'd begun to realize he wasn't joking. Maybe he never had been.

Too much.

How could that be true of anyone? Wasn't she who God made her to be? It wasn't like she was purposefully trying to push her own agenda... most of the time. Could she help being opinionated and decisive?

She tied her running shoes and turned back to the elevator.

"Where are you off to?" Laura wanted to know. She and Audrey were seated by the fireplace in the staff lounge.

Pam shrugged. "Going for a walk to get some fresh air before my shift starts."

Audrey's eyebrows shot up. "You're willingly going for a walk? Who are you, and what have you done with my friend Pam?"

"Hardy-har-har." Pam managed a grin. "It's a nice day, so why not? Besides, I walk."

"You wouldn't be going *with* someone, would you?" Laura's eyes narrowed.

"I've got to scoot, or I won't have time!" Pam slammed her palm against the elevator button. The door opened immediately, and she popped inside. As the doors closed, she heard Granger's name.

She hadn't fooled anyone. Why was she even trying?

Because she'd been too much for Mark, and one of these days, Granger would wake up and realize that Pam was not the cheerful, sunny person he deserved. He would also realize she was more than he wanted to deal with.

Baby steps.

Granger wasn't Mark, but Pam wasn't going to blindly fall for a man again without weighing out his good and bad qualities and determining if she could live with his flaws.

Yes, she had issues of her own. She wasn't blind enough to believe otherwise, but she'd learned to harness them somewhat since Mark left her that first time. She could have become the person, the wife, Mark needed if he hadn't died. That the children had perished with him remained the greatest injustice.

She blinked as the elevator doors opened.

Granger casually leaned against a nearby pillar as though he'd been waiting for hours. He straightened. "Oh, there you are!"

"I took five minutes," she pointed out.

His grin had become the best part of her days. No, maybe that belonged to his kisses. What was she doing, allowing those, when she was so uncertain they had a future? She should stop any pretense at a relationship before it went any further.

Instead, she accepted the hand he stretched out to her as they stepped outside a moment later. The air wasn't too chilly for late October, and she'd stuffed thin gloves into her jacket pockets. Holding Granger's hand was better, feeling his rough, warm palm against hers, feeling the gentle pressure of his fingers tightening around hers, feeling the strength he exuded.

Why couldn't she simply relax and see what happened?

Granger wasn't Mark. He wasn't a bit like Mark. Not in any way that mattered. But the rejection all those years ago still held her in a grip as strong as Granger's hand. Stronger, maybe, because throwing caution to the wind simply wasn't in her DNA.

Not after Mark.

Granger bumped her shoulder lightly. "Deep thoughts?"

Pam gave her head a shake, trying to dislodge her worries. "Trying not to."

He laughed. "I hear you. So, all these trees. How many acres of Christmas trees does Maranatha have, anyway?"

Pam tried to remember. "Twenty acres? Ish? I'm not sure, but Chris could tell you."

"Did you usually have a real tree in South Carolina?"

She let out a long breath. "I haven't put one up at all since the accident. Why bother, for just me? I was never home, anyway." Or as little as possible.

"I'm sorry. I keep blundering in there." Granger's arm came around her shoulders, and she missed the warmth of her hand in his.

"The memories are strong right now."

He rubbed her upper arm as they strolled along. "Memories can be a real bear."

Were they still talking about family matters? He was probably thinking of his military career.

"Does your knee keep you awake at night?"

"Sometimes. Keeping busy helps. That's why I'm hunting for projects around Jewel Lake. They take my mind off myself. I went into the army to help others, to help my country, and I'm still that man inside. The one who wants to make life better for others."

And in so doing, he'd given up his daughter. That was hard to reconcile, except he seemed to have believed that it was for Melissa's good. Maybe it had been. There was no way Pam could judge from here, even if it were her responsibility to do so.

It wasn't. Not by a long shot.

It had been hard enough falling in love at 23, when she hadn't felt fully formed. When the future seemed wide open, full of endless possibilities. When, with the optimism of youth, she and Mark had felt they could overcome anything at all because, hey, they were in love, and love conquered all.

Big surprise. It did not conquer all. At least, marital love didn't. God's love was a bit more ephemeral. It was hard to 'let go and let God,' as the saying went.

Pam wouldn't call herself ancient at 54, but she was definitely set in her ways. Her character was what it was, and anyone who couldn't deal with it need not stick around.

And yet, didn't the Bible talk about growing in knowledge and understanding? So maybe she didn't have any excuse for being stagnant. Stuck.

"I've never had a real tree."

Granger's musing brought Pam back to the moment with a mental thud.

"Not in my childhood, definitely not in deployment, and not even in Pennsylvania. I did buy a decent artificial one when I went on faculty at the Army War College."

"It's in storage? Or did you move everything west?"

"I sublet my condo in Carlisle, just in case Montana proved to be a very bad idea."

"And now?"

He looked down at Pam. His gaze was soft as he kissed her forehead. "It depends."

On her? But no. "You said things are going reasonably well with your daughter?"

"I think so, although I have nothing but decades of silence to compare it to. But I can't abandon her. Not again."

Time to pivot. "Well, if you're hankering for real trees, I know Julia is chomping at the bit to put them up all over the inn. I believe she mentioned 14 of them."

His eyes widened. "But there are already four artificial trees."

"Plus one in the staff lounge downstairs. You may not have noticed, but Julia is a wee, tiny bit crazy for Christmas."

"I knew I liked that woman."

Pam angled her eyebrows. "Oh?"

"Not that way, silly. Not the way I like you."

The grumble of an all-terrain vehicle became louder, accompanied by the happy woof of a dog.

Granger had missed his chance to kiss Pam... at least, for now.

A few seconds later the ATV lumbered around the curve with Chris onboard. She waved when she saw them and cut the engine. "Hey. Nice day for a walk." She looked between them as her dogs flopped down on the ground beside her.

"Sure is!"

"Has Julia picked the trees for the inn yet?" Pam asked.

Chris chuckled. "Yes, they're tagged. And I've been working on pricing the other trees we want to sell this year. I'm hopeful, considering the amount of interest we've seen."

An idea leaped into Granger's brain, fully formed, and he snapped his fingers. "Would the inn be willing to donate say, five or six trees to the Thanksgiving outreach at the church? Or maybe sell them at a discount..." He tapped his jaw.

"You'd have to talk to Julia about that, but I'm sure some deal could be arranged." Chris leaned forward on the handlebars. "What have you got in mind?"

Pam turned to him, a questioning look on her face.

"Or maybe a donation wouldn't be necessary." He tried to capture the images racing across his mind. "I was thinking some of the businesses in town might want to decorate trees, and we could give them out as door prizes to families who might otherwise have a lean Christmas."

"Sounds like a fun idea," Chris responded.

"What do you think?" he asked Pam.

She tightened her grip around his middle. When had she even placed her arm there, and how had he not noticed? Maybe she was staking her claim in Chris's presence, not that Granger had given her any indication his interest wasn't secure. "There would be details to be ironed out, but it's a way to get their name out in the town and do something good for others. They could always write off the decor — and the tree, for that matter — as a business expense. We just wouldn't want the ornaments to be too commercial, but something that would appeal to families. To children."

"Right, right." Granger nodded. "All that. We could line them up in the church foyer and people could vote on their top three favorites as they came in for the banquet."

"Depending on how many we're seating, they'd be attractive around the perimeter of the room. Will the banquet be held in the academy's gymnasium? That seems the biggest space, if not the most beautiful. But a row of trees would help lend a festive air without a lot of extra work."

"I like how you think, woman." He tapped her nose. Then remembered Chris sitting astride the ATV, watching them. "Well, that's one more idea to spin past Marshall when we meet tomorrow."

"You're all in with Christmas and with the church?" Chris asked.

"Sure." Granger shrugged. "I need to be useful, and I've got nothing better to do. Why not?"

"Why not, indeed?" Chris murmured. "If you want to have a look at the trees, the taller ones are on the west side, below the bluff. The younger trees are over that way, with alternating rows of pines, spruces, and firs."

"Do we have time to look around?" Granger asked Pam.

She blinked and glanced at her watch. "Not today, I'm afraid. Darla will be starting in 15 minutes, so I need to get back to the kitchen. Maybe another time."

"Sure, whenever you like." Chris reached for the key.

"Hey, come down for dinner?" Pam asked.

Chris shrugged. "Not today. I've got a lot going on up here."

"Okay, but don't be a stranger."

"I won't." Chris waved, revved the engine, and sped away between the trees, the dogs loping behind her.

Reluctantly, Granger turned back toward the inn. "Has she not been around much?"

"No, and I wish she would. Her quietness is a nice counterpoint to Audrey and Laura." She clapped her hand over her mouth. "Oops, forget I said that."

Granger chuckled. "My lips are sealed." They wanted to be sealed over Pam's, but she was right about the shortage of time. "You ladies all seem so different from each other. How did you get to be friends, anyway?"

"Julia, of course. She's always had that attractive, inviting way about her. People just want to be around her. She listens. She cares. She makes everyone feel special. She's like Mary Poppins."

Granger blinked. "I must have missed a transition."

"Sorry. I forgot you weren't around kids much. In the movie, Mary Poppins is practically perfect in every way."

"Julia is very nice," Granger began cautiously. "But I never once have looked at her and wondered if she were ready to date. I know she's a fairly recent widow."

"Two years now." Pam clamped her mouth shut.

And Granger was forever putting his foot in it. "And then I caught the way the guy down the road looks at her, and I'm thinking no man ought to stand in his way. When she's ready, she'll find Monte waiting for her."

"That's what I think, too. She keeps insisting Monte and George were best friends, and that Monte promised George he'd keep an eye out for her before George died. But Monte's not looking out for her like a man with no endgame."

"So, Julia gathered friends around her in college?"

"She did. She roomed with Chris that first year. Wendy and Audrey had been childhood friends, as unlikely as that seems. Wendy befriended me. Audrey pulled in Laura. And here we are again, decades later. There's nothing that makes a woman feel old faster than seeing how her friends have aged."

"Not a gray hair between you."

"Hair dye has its uses."

Why hadn't he ever thought of that? "You, too?"

"Absolutely. Those gray roots already had a firm grip before the accident. I would have been snow white in no time if I hadn't taken matters into my own hands. A gray-haired woman gets no respect in the business world. Lucky Chris still has her natural color, I think."

"Huh." Hadn't there been a few older women on staff at Carlisle? But maybe Pam was right, that people — men, especially — thought of women differently based on their hair color.

They'd arrived back at the inn, and Darla's car was already parked in the staff lot off to the side. Granger might not have made use of the hour to kiss this woman, but it wasn't a waste. They'd definitely gotten to know each other better.

And he had a great idea for the outreach event.

Win, win.

Fourteen

M ay I have everyone's attention, please?"

Pam took in Wendy's poised demeanor as she stood beside the kitchen door at Maranatha. Who knew Wendy would be in her element in front of a crowd? Or... did this qualify as a crowd? In Pam's eyes, 49 people definitely did.

She was just here to make sure the foodie end ran well. Okay, maybe to support Wendy and keep an eye on Granger, as well. He was at the far table with Oliver, who danced eagerly around the table, waiting not so patiently for his instructions.

Wendy held up two pieces of shaped gingerbread. "You'll see we've already baked the pieces for your structure. You'll find royal icing and an assortment of candies at your tables, as well as a basic assembly diagram. Let me show you how to attach the pieces to each other."

From another table, Maggie Johannesson smiled brightly at Pam and beckoned her over. Monte's sister, Sheryl, had brought her granddaughter for the event.

Pam drifted closer as Wendy demonstrated, but she didn't want to distract the girl from paying attention. When Wendy gave the go-ahead, Pam closed the gap. "Hi, you two! Ready to make your masterpiece?"

"So ready!" Maggie bounced on her heels. "Ours will be the best."

"You might be right, but it looks like you will have stiff competition."

Maggie waved a dismissive hand. "Oliver is just a little kid, and Sidney didn't even come. She probably knew she couldn't make as nice a one as me."

"Maggie!" Sheryl cautioned.

"Sorry. I'm not supposed to trash talk." Not that Maggie looked contrite. "Do you know the women from Happy Trails? Sometimes I get to go horseback riding there."

Happy Trails Stable was the business at the bottom of the Maranatha Inn driveway, but Pam had never turned in there. "No, I haven't met them. Are they here?"

"Yeah! That's Ms. Emma. She's my teacher. And there's Ms. Vivienne and Ms. Alexia. They're sisters! And you know what? They have *six* older brothers."

"Wow! Nine kids! That's a big family." And Granger had seemed shocked by Wendy's six.

Sheryl chuckled. "For those who are only children, it does seem big, for sure. It's a case of his, hers, and theirs."

"That makes a little more sense, though it's possible the other way, too." Not that Pam would know. She'd never aspired to having more than two. When she and Mark had welcomed a daughter, then a son, to their family, they'd easily agreed their family was complete.

"Ms. Emma is dating Mr. McDiarmid, so she can't be my new mom." Maggie still seemed to be eyeing the table where the three 20-something women worked together.

"Maggie." Sheryl's voice was stern. "What did we say about that at home?"

The child offered a dramatic sigh. "I'm not allowed to ask women to date Dad and be my new mom."

Pam stifled a laugh. "Seriously?"

"You would not believe her nerve." Sheryl shook her head.

"I want a new mom. Is that so terrible? My mom died when I was a baby." Maggie studied Pam. "But I think you're too old to marry my dad."

"I'm pretty sure I am about your grandmother's age."

Wendy paused by the table. "Did you have questions about the first steps on assembling your gingerbread house?"

Maggie blinked and reached for two walls. "Nope. I just got busy talking. It happens sometimes."

This kid. Pam turned away. She refused to look at Granger, but she could meet their neighbors. She stopped beside the table with the three young women. "Hi! I'm Pam Whorley, the chef here at Maranatha. I hear you are sisters and own Happy Trails?"

"That's us! I'm Alexia, and this is my twin, Emma, and our older sister, Vivienne. Do you like riding horseback?"

"I've never been on a horse in my life."

"Ooh, we should remedy that! We've got some perfect horses for beginners, and the trails are so beautiful… even at this time of year, when most of the leaves have fallen, but the snow hasn't come yet."

"If I get bored, I'll keep that in mind."

The other twin glanced at Pam with a smile. "I saw you were talking to Maggie. Did she ask you to be her new mom?"

Pam chuckled. "Nope. She declared me too old. Which is not incorrect."

"Lucky you. I'm a teacher at Creekside Academy, and she's asked me like three times."

"She mentioned you have a boyfriend, so maybe she'll relent, now?"

"One can only hope." Emma eyed her snickering sisters. "Don't laugh. One of these days she'll realize you two are single, as well. Just you wait."

"Not happening." Vivienne smoothed royal icing on the edge of a gingerbread slab.

"Ditto." Alexia ran her fingers through the candy bowl.

"The poor girl appears doomed to disappointment."

The younger women laughed. "Seems so," agreed Emma.

Pam stopped at a couple of other tables to meet folks she'd seen at church and in the community. Finally, Granger and Oliver were the last ones left. It would draw even more attention if she ignored them, right?

Oliver's tongue poked out of the side of his mouth as he focused on getting the icing where he wanted it. Looked like this gingerbread house might be a wee bit messier than some of the others, but good on Granger for letting the boy do it.

"Hey, Pam." Granger's voice was like velvet.

"Hi, yourself. How's the gingerbread house going, Oliver?"

"Good…" The slab slid to the table in slow motion. The boy sighed. "Not so good."

"Here, let me hold it until the icing dries." Granger set the wall back into position before glancing back at Pam. "Aren't you making one?"

"Me? No."

"But you should. It's fun."

"I see how much fun it is."

Humor glimmered in Granger's eyes. "More than you could ever imagine. Methinks the real fun will be turning this kid loose to decorate it with all the candies."

"All the candies?" Oliver smeared icing unevenly over another piece. "I thought they were for eating."

"You didn't get enough sugar at Halloween last week?"

"Never enough." Oliver focused as he set the new wall in place.

It might have helped if more of the icing were on the edges and less in the middle, but Pam wasn't going to be the one to rain on his parade. Wendy had made plenty of icing for each table, so it wasn't like they'd run out. Probably.

"I like sweet things, myself." But Granger was watching Pam.

"People can be sweeter than candy." He puckered his lips in her direction.

"Hmm." Oliver clearly wasn't paying attention to his grandfather.

Good thing. Pam's cheeks had warmed and, by the gleam in Granger's eyes, he'd noticed.

Look at him, flirting like a teenager!

Everything had sped so quickly with Denise back in his youth that he'd missed this delicious feeling of anticipation. It had gone *too* quickly, obviously, since she hadn't been nearly as invested in their future as he'd been.

On the other hand, she was still married to Grant 35 years later, so maybe the fault lay more with Granger than with Denise.

He refocused on his grandson. That water was so far under the bridge it had, no doubt, circled the Pacific Ocean several times over the years. Nothing good could come of trying to determine what had gone wrong.

They'd been kids. He'd been ready to deploy. He'd wanted a sweetheart waiting at home for him, but that had never happened. Denise had moved on before she even gave birth to Granger's daughter.

Water under the bridge.

Focus on the here and now. A morning of bonding with his grandson. Of seeing Pam and Wendy in their elements… not that he'd spent more than ten seconds thinking about Wendy, other than noticing she'd truly come into her own leading this event.

Which meant he could trust her input on the outreach dinner. Not that he'd mistrusted her, exactly, but he didn't know her, and home-school fundraisers weren't the same thing as what she'd be doing in her role at Maranatha. Pam had said that, in addition to managing events for the inn, Wendy was in charge of social media. She and Laura also handled most of the housekeeping. While there were more guests in and out these days, it still wasn't the bustling proposition Julia had hoped for.

Or so he thought, though he'd never asked. It wasn't any of his business.

Pam was his business.

No, Oliver and Sidney and their mother were. He couldn't woo Pam at the expense of his daughter's family. But why would there be any conflict? Melissa was still reeling from Chad's defection. She was certainly not in the market to remarry, but that didn't necessarily mean she'd be against him doing so.

He stilled, his hand poised above the candy bowl.

He was thinking of marrying Pam? Since when? She'd been easing her way into his heart for an entire month now. Somehow, she now owned it.

"Those red candies are yummy."

Granger blinked at Oliver's voice and pulled back his hand. The kid was eyeing him like he'd lost it. Maybe he had. "I'm sure they are."

"Am I doing a good job?"

"Sure are, buddy." The lie slid out of Granger's mouth. The structure leaned to the left like it yearned to embrace the table.

Oliver studied it. "It's gonna fall over."

"You think?"

"Yeah. I'm no good at this stuff."

"Sure, you are. It's just that you've never done this before, right? Lots of things take practice." Was it leaning even further? Looked like it. Maybe intervention would be required. "Want me to see if I can help?"

"Yeah." Oliver backed up, both hands in the air. "I'm just making a mess."

Laughter came from a nearby table, and Granger glanced over to see a fully collapsed creation. Its builders seemed to think it was hilarious.

Granger nudged his grandson. "Go ask them how they're going to fix it, Ollie."

"I don't know them."

"That's how we get to know people. By talking to them."

"You do it, Gramps."

"We'll go together." Granger eyed their own structure. Would it still be standing in five minutes? Well, theirs wasn't the first to collapse. "Come on."

Wendy headed over as the three young women giggled uncontrollably. "Oh, no! What happened?"

"Lex is what happened," one of them gasped out.

"Hey, Viv is the one who put the roof on before the icing was set."

The icing was supposed to set in between? Granger must have skimmed that part of the instructions. He'd probably been thinking about Pam.

"I'm curious, too," Granger interjected. "Ours is leaning hard to starboard. How can we fix it?"

The young women chortled even harder.

"Oh, no!" Wendy wrung her hands. "Maybe I made the icing wrong." She glanced at the other tables.

So did Granger... but everyone else seemed to be faring just fine. At least he and Oliver weren't the only ones with troubles, though.

Pam materialized at Granger's side. "Maybe if we get some cans or something to put on the leaning side to prop it up until it sets better? That should even work on this fully collapsed one."

One of the women gasped for air. "Only you, Lex."

"Hey! You were here, too. It's not all my fault."

"Cans sound good. We'll give you a hand." Anything to spend a minute with Pam. "Come on, Ollie."

They followed Pam through the kitchen to a large walk-in pantry, where she loaded their arms with cans.

"We might need a strap of sorts, too. At least, for the Cavanagh sisters' one." Pam looked around the pantry. "I wonder how their icing got soft. Hmm. Oh, here's some kitchen twine. Not perfect, but it will have to do." She grabbed a roll.

"Take your load to the ladies' table, Ollie."

"Okay." The boy went through the double swinging doors.

Granger turned back to Pam. "You're amazing."

"I'm really not." She laughed. "But thank you for thinking so. I'm not sure this will work to salvage the construction."

"How come this is Wendy's thing and not yours?"

Her face straightened in an instant. "Maybe because she's the kind of attentive mother I never was? I was always working, too busy to do silly little projects like this with my kids. And then my chances were gone."

Oh, man. Granger should have kept his mouth shut. "I'm sorry." He tried to hold her gaze, but she wouldn't look him in the eye. If he didn't have an armload, he'd... never mind. He set the cans down and reached for her. "Come here."

Pam stepped into his embrace and wrapped her arms around his back. She clung to him but didn't look up.

"Hey, sweetheart. I shouldn't have joked about that. I'm sorry."

"It's okay. You couldn't have known how raw that wound still is."

So raw that she wasn't ready to move on even after a dozen years? It wasn't like she was young enough to have more children, even if she'd once harbored that hope. And given Sidney's attitude, his grandkids were more of a negative reminder than positive.

She pushed back out of his arms with a fleeting smile. "Let's go. We have a construction crisis to overcome."

Was that how she viewed all of life? One thing after another that needed to be held together by any means possible?

CHAPTER

Fifteen

P raise to the Lord, the Almighty, the King of creation!"

Pam sat halfway to the back of Creekside Fellowship with Chris on one side of her and Wendy on the other. Maybe if she kept watching Granger's blurring hands as he drummed along with the worship team, she could ignore the lyrics of the peppy song. Because the words to that second verse taunted her.

Praise to the Lord, above all things so wondrously reigning...

It sure hadn't felt like God was in control that November day 12 years ago, let alone wondrously so.

Sheltering you under His wings, and so gently sustaining...

Pam blinked back tears. She would not cry in church. Not this many years later. Had God sheltered and sustained her back then? Probably. She would likely have been in much worse shape in those dark days without God, but she hadn't felt any specific comfort like this song projected.

Have you not seen all that is needful has been sent by His gracious ordaining?

Had God supplied all her needs? Sort of? She'd survived, after all. The third verse began, and Pam braced herself. All this praise was wearing on her. And yes, she felt guilt because of it.

Praise to the Lord, who will prosper your work and defend you; surely His goodness and mercy shall daily attend you.

That reminded her of the end of Psalm 23. *Surely goodness and mercy shall follow me all the days of my life, and I shall dwell in the house of the Lord forever.*

Wouldn't a merciful God have spared her family? At least spared her children?

Ponder anew what the Almighty can do, if with His love He befriends you…

Maybe that was the problem. She hadn't felt befriended by God. Loved by God. She believed in Him, for sure, but it all seemed so impersonal. It had before that tragic day, and God had seemed even less approachable since then. She'd done her part, hadn't she? She'd kept her faith. She'd tried to hold onto the belief that God had a plan.

A plan to leave her all alone with no more chances to make amends with Mark. With no opportunity to become a better mother.

Ponder anew?

Pam squeezed her eyes hard again, trying not to draw attention to herself in this pew full of women who'd known her when she was young and optimistic. Laura's strong, beautiful alto rang out from the other side of Wendy as though she believed and lived every one of these words of tribute.

Praise to the Lord! O let all that is in me adore Him! All that has life and breath, come now with praises before Him.

She had life and breath. Mark didn't. Courtney and Roderick didn't. Pam was the only one in her family left to bring praises before God. And she didn't want to. She didn't trust God.

Granger should run away now. Or, she should.

God didn't want good things for Pam, and Granger was too good to be true.

But she'd tried. She had! How could one be good enough for God?

Oh, she knew the answer. Knew that all had sinned and come

short of God's glory. Knew that there was no one righteous, not even one. She knew that Jesus had come to stand in the gap to save her.

But where was the hope? Where was the joy, the love, the peace?

Nowhere, that's where. Not for her, anyway. She'd tried.

Pam should never have come to Montana, especially not during the Advent season, especially not to Christmas-crazy Julia Cox's inn. Even the name Maranatha meant 'Come, Lord Jesus,' the same definition as the Latin word *adventus*. How had she thought she could function here?

The song ended, the congregation took their seats. So did the worship team, and the pastor prayed.

This seemed to be a church where gratitude was preached all the way through November. How could Pam be thankful for the loss of her family? It went against every grain in her body. It felt sacrilegious.

No, God had used — was still using — that event to punish her. There was nothing to be thankful for in being singled out for His chastisement.

Had she been, though? Her conscience niggled.

Maybe not compared to people in war-torn areas. People who were dying inch-by-inch from starvation.

So, she should be thankful for her own circumstances.

Thankful she didn't have it as bad as some others did? That wasn't gratitude. That was relief.

Wendy wiggled on the pew beside Pam, bumping her elbow against Pam's. If there were any room, Pam would shift away, but Chris was tight on her other side. They were packed in here like sardines. Claustrophobia choked her.

She needed air. She needed space. She needed… something, anything, that didn't remind her of Mark's car, flattened in the accident. She should never have looked at it. Even now, the image was scorched on her retinas. No space had remained for their fragile bodies.

Pam pulled to her feet. "Excuse me," she whispered at Chris. The other direction was closer to an aisle, but it was easier to slip past Chris and Audrey and Julia than Wendy.

"You okay?" Julia whispered.

Pam didn't reply. She stared down at the worn carpet as she scurried toward the back of the sanctuary and into the foyer. She hesitated an instant then registered Loretta and Vance Satterfield, the inn's most regular guests, standing at the window. Pam veered for the restrooms.

Why hadn't she brought her own car today? The parking lot wasn't huge, and it seemed a waste of fuel. She'd come with Chris and Wendy, and now she was stuck waiting for the end of the service.

She could call a taxi.

Right, and face even more concerned questioning later at the inn. That was coming, regardless, unless she resumed her place as though she'd simply needed to use the facilities. Then she might only get Audrey's homily on how pelvic floor exercises could help mitigate the sense of urgency.

Pam could do without that, but it was too late. She could pretend she'd been sick, but she'd never been a liar and wasn't about to start now.

She locked herself in a stall and held back her tears. This wasn't the time or the place. She didn't need blotchy makeup or any other evidence that she couldn't hold herself together.

The restroom door creaked open. "Pamela?" Loretta Satterfield's sweet Southern voice rang out. "You okay, peach?"

"Just fine. Thanks, Loretta."

By the silence that followed, Pam was willing to bet that the other woman wasn't buying it. But Pam was not giving in.

144

When Granger resumed his seat on the drum throne for the closing song, his gaze latched unerringly on the pew where the Maranatha Inn women were sitting. There was a slight gap between Wendy and Chris.

Hadn't Pam been sitting there? Where was she?

His body fell into rhythm as his eyes skimmed the pews for any glimpse of her, but she wasn't in the sanctuary.

He'd found Eli's sermon on gratitude in all circumstances to be uplifting. Challenging, to be sure, but also encouraging. Knowing how raw Pam's emotions were, he'd prayed for her, trusting the Lord to spread a soothing salve over her wounds. If she could get the gist of the young preacher's words, his heart for the hurting, she'd find peace in her soul.

Right? He'd believed it. Prayed it, all through Eli's confession of how difficult his young years had been in foster care, how God had found him and saved him and called him to ministry.

When had Pam slipped out? Early in the sermon, or two minutes ago? Granger didn't know, because he'd been sitting in the first pew next to the worship leader, Caleb, and his wife.

Maybe she was in the restroom. But somehow, in the depths of his being, Granger suspected her absence was caused by something more than a call of nature. He drummed out the closing song's grand finale then stilled the cymbals when young Eli returned to the mic for the benediction and closing prayer.

"May I leave you today with words from Psalm nine? 'I will praise you, Lord, with all my heart; I will tell of all the marvelous things you have done. I will be filled with joy because of you. I will sing praises to your name, O Most High.' Go forth, and tell of God's marvelous deeds!"

He'd taken two steps off the platform when Oliver, running in from children's church, slammed into his body. "Gramps, there's Ms. Wendy!"

Granger ruffled his grandson's hair. "You're right. Do you want to say hi?"

The boy nodded. "And thank you, because Mom really likes

the gingerbread house. She said it was unique. And artful. What does artful mean, Gramps?"

"Full of art."

Oliver nodded. "In this case, that means full of candy, I think. Can I say thanks?"

"Sure, go for it." Granger ambled behind the boy. At least this gave him a good excuse to get near the Maranatha women without it being weird. Which was also ridiculous, since he was pretty sure they all knew he and Pam met in the lobby nearly every evening after she closed the kitchen. Julia and Laura did, at least.

Oliver was talking to Wendy, his hands waving so much he nearly whacked a passerby in the belly. Thankfully, the older man grinned and gave Ollie a wide berth.

Granger paused a few feet back to allow the boy his autonomy, and Julia stepped to his side. "Hi, Granger."

"Hi." He hesitated. "Where did Pam go?"

Julia's brows furrowed together as she bit her lip. "I'm not sure. She slipped out quite a while ago."

Granger's heart sank. Maybe the sermon had sent her scurrying before she'd heard the redemptive parts.

"She looked upset, but I didn't want to make things worse by following her. Maybe I should have…"

He shook his head. "It's hard to know. She'll be okay." He glanced over to see Oliver still in earnest conversation with Wendy. He pulled his phone from his pocket. No message from Pam, not that he'd expected there to be.

Granger: *Hey! Want to get lunch with me?*

That wasn't exactly what he wanted to say, but if she agreed, maybe he'd find out more of what was going on inside her head.

Pam: *Thanks, but not today.*

His index finger hovered over the tiny keyboard. How to reply?

Granger: *We could go for a walk later if you like?*

Pam: *I'm not feeling great. I think I need a lowkey afternoon in my room.*

He was striking out.

Granger: *Okay, but if you change your mind, shoot me a text. I'd love to spend time with you.*

And then... nothing. No response. He chomped on his lip.

"No luck?"

Right. He was standing in the middle of the aisle in Creekside Fellowship talking to Julia as the sanctuary emptied around them. "She wants some time alone."

"Hmm." Julia looked thoughtful. "She gets in her own head sometimes."

"Don't we all?" He tried for a light laugh. Likely failed.

"That's true, but I think Pam's has a spiral slide inside it."

"She's not..." He glanced around and lowered his voice to a bare whisper. "Suicidal?"

"No, I don't think so. She might've had those thoughts after the accident, but I don't think so anymore. But it's a tough spot."

This was information he wasn't sure he wanted to have. Pam seemed so strong until a moment like this. But that strength, that independence, could also be an armor. A facade. He'd had some glimpses to the tender heart inside, but she was shoring up her defenses again.

Just like Melissa.

And Sidney.

And what was a man like Granger to do about it? He'd been career military. His life had contained more blunt force than tender finesse. He didn't know how to pussyfoot around women's emotions.

He'd failed with Denise, and it hadn't gotten any easier, any clearer, since then.

What was he even thinking, trying to establish relationships? Trying to make a difference?

He couldn't walk away from his daughter again. By extension, he was in his granddaughter's life for the long haul.

But Granger didn't owe anything to Pamela Whorley. If she pushed him aside, he had no choice but to give her whatever space she demanded. They'd barely begun to explore a relationship, yet Granger's brain had leaped over all the obstacles to envision them together for the remainder of their years.

His brain might think he was Superman, leaping tall buildings with a single bound, but ignoring the hindrances and pretending they didn't exist wouldn't work. There were landmines. Walls. Coils of barbed wire. Mud pits. Aerial obstacles. Each had to be dealt with in turn and overcome.

After Denise, Granger had known he couldn't handle another relationship. He'd steered clear for all these years. Somehow, Pam had crept around his defenses and caught his attention. He'd been lulled to believe that he was a more mature man than back then, that he could make a relationship work now.

But females were still emotional creatures, and women in their fifties, while being much more mature than 20-somethings, had also been shaped by life's difficulties.

It would be easier not to fall in love.

That ship had sailed.

CHAPTER
Sixteen

Tap. Tap. Tap.

Pam stared at her closed door.

"Want to talk?" Wendy's voice.

Wasn't it clearly evident that the answer was no?

"Audrey and Laura drove into Missoula for the afternoon. Julia is at the front desk. It's just you and me down here."

Pam shook her head, not that her friend could see through the slab door.

"I want to stay angry with Dave, you know? I mean, I get why he fell out of love with me, but don't wedding vows count for anything? He promised the whole gamut: in sickness, in health, for richer, for poorer. You attended our wedding. You heard him. But then he wouldn't even go to counseling. Said he'd 'moved on.' How do you make promises and then 'move on?'"

Great. Wendy was making this all about her. Couldn't she appreciate Pam needing a moment of her own? Because now Pam felt guilty for shutting her friend out. Was that Wendy's goal, or had her own hurt resurfaced because of the church service, too?

God?

But God remained as silent as He'd been for years. If Pam were being honest, she hadn't really felt His presence since Bible school. Not in that heady rush kind of way where it felt like with God at her side, she could conquer absolutely anything. They were a team, the two of them.

Then her busy, all-encompassing career. Mark, with his shaky faith. The kids, who'd been colicky babies and tantrum-prone toddlers, but the daycare had mostly dealt with that. Then the sense of her life slowly unraveling as Mark became distant, exposing that God had done the same.

"Pam?"

She glared at the door. *I need some alone time.* Courtney's hormonally charged, tween voice echoed in Pam's head. Was it too petulant to say the words out loud at 54 years old?

"Okay, I won't bother you anymore."

Pam's heart squeezed. Would cradling her pain and ignoring Wendy's help her get past it? It hadn't so far. Neither had the distraction of hard work or trying to outrun it. "Come in."

The knob turned but stopped. "Are you sure?"

Not at all. "Yeah. I'll put on some tea." She stood and turned toward the kitchenette.

Wendy entered Pam's suite and glanced around before marching across the space and flinging the drapes wide. "It's dark in here. It's a beautiful day, and you need sunlight."

Pam gritted her teeth. If she'd wanted sunlight, she'd have swept the coverings aside herself. She filled her kettle and turned it on, battling with her emotions.

Drat menopause, anyway. She'd somehow managed to deal with her monthly ups and downs, but the past couple of years had tossed a curveball into that. More like a grenade. She'd always resisted medication, but would hormone therapy keep these deep dives at bay? Maybe it would be worth it.

Or maybe she deserved to wallow.

But now she sounded like Wendy. She couldn't encourage Wendy without practicing what she preached, could she? Talk about two-faced.

Pam peered into her tea box. "I have Earl Grey, chamomile, or green tea. What's your preference?"

"Hmm. Green, if you have honey."

"I take my tea and coffee black. Sorry."

"I have honey in my room. I'll be right back." Wendy slipped out the door.

Pam sighed. She should have known. A minute later she'd poured the tea and Wendy had fixed hers to her liking. Now they sat facing each other in the two easy chairs in front of the French doors. Neither was in direct sunlight due to the deck off the main floor above, so whew for that.

She took a sip of her tea. If Wendy wanted her to talk, good luck. She'd have to work for it.

"I had a text from Selah after church."

Pam waited.

Wendy twisted her mug in her hands. "She said Shyanne went to a work conference and had an affair."

Shyanne was Dave's trophy wife. Didn't sound like much of a prize now. "I'm sorry." For what? Pam didn't know. Maybe for Wendy's pain.

"I wonder if they'll separate. He shouldn't put up with that."

"I guess that's their problem."

"How can you say that? It affects my kids!"

"Sorry. That's true. You heard from Selah, not Faith?" Faith was the high-schooler living with her father, after all. Selah was away at college.

"I wonder if I should call Faith."

Pam had nothing to give. She'd never raised children to adulthood. "I can't answer that."

"Maybe I'll give her a day or two. Or will she feel like I don't care? It's hard to be so far away."

"Faith probably doesn't even know Selah told you."

"Also true." Wendy set her teacup down. "I should go home."

"But you've got a whole bunch of events planned here into the new year. You can't leave Julia in the lurch for those. And although I feel for your kids — Faith, especially — it's an issue with their father. I hate to say it, but you're not part of either the problem or the solution."

Wendy darted her a glance. "I maybe could be."

What? Pam stared at her. "I'm not following."

"Maybe… never mind."

"No, tell me."

"I don't know. It's probably silly, but maybe Dave would see me differently now. He has to know I would never, ever cheat on him."

"Do you hear yourself right now?"

"Yes?"

"Dave had more than one affair while he was married to you. He threw you out like last week's trash. You can't possibly think it would be a good idea to give him another chance to hurt you?"

"Maybe he wouldn't."

"And probably he would. Did Selah put this in your head? Is there *any* reason to believe he's changed?"

Wendy's jaw quivered. "No, but marriage is sacred."

"Wendy. He broke his vows. He divorced you years ago. It's over. Totally, completely, irrevocably over." As it should be, the cheating scum.

"But sometimes God salvages broken things. Haven't you heard Sheryl and Ted's story? They were divorced for 18 years, but they're back together. They're proof."

Pam shook her head. "Neither of them had an affair or remarried in the intervening years. It's not the same."

"I guess. I just… I feel like such a total failure. I mean, look at me." Wendy gestured down her body. "But Dave once loved me anyway."

"You're not a total failure. You're an amazing woman, and you did a fabulous job leading the gingerbread house workshop yesterday. I have no doubt your other events will be just as creative."

Wendy managed a smile. "Granger's grandson talked to me

after church. He was dancing all over the place while he thanked me for yesterday. He said his mom really liked the house."

"See?"

"I know, but… no, you wouldn't understand. You're so put together. You don't unravel at the seams like I do. I mean, look at you. You're trim and petite even though you're constantly surrounded by amazing food. I only have to look at a plate and I gain five pounds. Even if it's a plate of dry lettuce."

"I don't have it together." But the admission hurt.

"Puh-leeze. I'm the one who's a disaster."

Could Pam reveal the churning beneath her calm surface? If not now, with Wendy, when, and with whom? Granger knew a little… and it was better if he didn't figure out any more.

"That was a nice dinner, Dad. Thanks." Melissa leaned back in her chair.

"You're welcome." Granger grinned. "I don't have a huge repertoire, but I do like to cook some. I've missed that, staying at the inn."

"I didn't even know macaroni and cheese didn't always come from a box!" Oliver's eyes were bright.

"I like the box one better," Sidney mumbled.

"Sidney!"

"Well, it's true." The girl surged to her feet and seemed to catch her mother's expression. "Thanks for the effort, Gramps."

Granger would take it. "You're welcome. What would you like me to make next time?"

She shrugged. "I don't care."

"Sidney, you're being rude."

"Look, I'm putting my plate in the dishwasher." Sidney opened the appliance with a flourish worthy of Vanna White and set her plate and utensils in place. "See? I'm wonderful." Then she sashayed from the room.

"What do I do with her?" Melissa shook her head. "I don't have a clue."

"I have no idea, and that's mostly because I wasn't around when you were that age. I'm sorry."

"I'm pretty sure Mom didn't let me get away with that kind of attitude."

"You could ground her!" Oliver said eagerly.

"Little pitchers have big ears." Granger reached over and ruffled his grandson's hair.

The boy frowned. "What does that mean?"

Melissa rose from the table and began stacking plates. "Never mind, kid. Do you have any homework for school? Any forms I need to sign?"

"Just my journal." Oliver kicked at the table leg, but then his face brightened. "I can draw a picture of my gingerbread house for my entry!"

"Sounds like a plan. First, wipe the table, then get your journal out."

"Okay. I need the gel pens, too."

"Go for it."

Granger stayed seated as Oliver and Melissa moved around the kitchen.

"Thanks again for cooking tonight, Dad. You usually have dinner at the inn, don't you?"

He did, partly because guests received a discount, and partly because he couldn't get enough of seeing Pam at work. But after she'd blown him off this afternoon, he wasn't sure what to do. Inviting himself to Melissa's had been an easy solution, albeit temporary.

The big question was whether he'd wait by the fireside after her shift tonight.

Scratch that. The big question was whether she'd rush on past or not, but he'd be there.

"So, I heard a rumor about you."

"Oh?" But Granger's gut tightened. "What kind of rumor?"

"That you're dating the chef from the inn."

"We've... uh... gone out a couple of times."

"How come I'm the last to know?"

"I'm pretty sure you're not the last. No one put an announcement in the Jewel Lake Gazette that I've noticed."

She waved her hand in dismissal. "You know what I mean."

Granger wasn't being fair to his daughter. She deserved better from him. "You're right. I just wasn't sure what you'd think about it, and it's all so new that I'm not sure what I think about it, either."

"What's new?" Oliver plunked his spiral-bound notebook on the table along with a basket of gel pens.

Granger exchanged a grin with his daughter over the boy's head. The kid didn't miss much, but at least it didn't seem like Melissa was upset about the idea. "Your old gramps has gone on a date. Do you know what that is?"

The boy's nose wrinkled. "Smooching?"

Granger gulped. "It might involve smooching, but it really means choosing to spend time with someone you like."

"Oh. Like you taking me to make a gingerbread house because you like me."

"Sort of." Granger was going to leave it right there. Any more details could come from Melissa. He looked at her. "You okay with it?"

"Sure. You've been solo a long time, and it's not like you're getting back together with Mom." She grimaced, her expression so similar to Ollie's that Granger bit back a laugh. "So long as no one is asking me to go out, it's fine."

"It's been a couple of years."

"Don't remind me."

Granger shrugged.

"Want to bring your lady friend by sometime?"

"Maybe? I'm just not sure if things are going to work out.

She's only made a three-month commitment there, and one of those is already past."

"I guess it's your job to make sure she wants to stay beyond that."

"Maybe..." Granger took a deep breath. "Maybe I'm not sure of my own long-term welcome here."

His daughter's brows furrowed. "Are you talking about me?"

He glanced at Ollie, who was drawing the crooked outline of a crooked gingerbread house, his tongue poking out the side of his mouth. "Maybe?"

"Are you thinking of returning to Pennsylvania? I thought this was for real."

"I've sublet my place there. I told you that. I wasn't sure how things would pan out when I came."

"But now?"

"Do you want me?"

Oliver paused and looked between them.

"Yes," Melissa said.

Granger could feel one burden rolling off his shoulders. "Then I'll make plans to stay. I'll start looking for a house next week."

"That easy?"

"You're my top priority, honey. You and the kids. I messed up big time letting your mother push me aside way back when, and I want nothing more than to stay involved now." Even though that doubtless meant facing Denise in person at some point in the future. A worry for another day.

"Well, good. Glad we've got that settled."

"Me, too." He grinned at her.

"What's settled?" Ollie asked.

"Gramps is staying in Jewel Lake."

"In our house? He can share my room."

Granger couldn't resist mussing the kid's hair one more time. "Thanks, but you snore. I'll get my own place, but we'll see each other often."

"I don't snore. That was you."

"Never!"

Melissa laughed. "You're so good with him."

Granger cut his gaze to the hallway then turned back to his daughter with his eyebrows raised.

She sighed. "No one is good with the other one right now. You're definitely not alone… but I think it's helpful, all the same."

"I appreciate that."

Now if only Pam would be as happy about his decision as Melissa and Oliver were. Because he was just as committed to her as he was to his family.

CHAPTER
Seventeen

The dinner shift had been busy enough that Pam's brain didn't have time to wander. But now Darla had clocked out for the evening, leaving the dining room tidy and ready for the breakfast shift.

Now, Pam eyed the back stairs. It was tempting to take the easy way, even though it meant threading through the laundry and utility rooms. But since when was she chicken? She'd always faced life head-on. Unflinching. Sometimes to her detriment.

She'd run out from church this morning. She'd blown Granger off for lunch. She'd tried to block Wendy out of her space, but that hadn't worked.

Was Granger waiting in the lobby? That was the current question.

Her heart said he was. Her head said he was smart enough to cut his losses and escape while the going was good. He'd figured out she was too much to deal with, and who could blame him?

Pam got after Wendy for talking smack about herself, but she was doing it to herself, too. *It takes one to know one.* She flinched then braced her shoulders. If Granger wasn't in the lobby, she'd have her answer.

She slipped out of the kitchen, then passed through the dining room to the front desk. Julia always locked the doors at ten and dimmed the lighting. The fireplace beyond flickered, and Granger's head lifted.

He hadn't given up on her.

Yet.

Not every man was like Mark or Dave.

Granger rose to his feet. "Hey, Pam. How was your day?"

He was going to play this as normal. She let out a breath she hadn't realized she'd been holding. "I've had better; I've had worse."

He nodded. "I made you a hot chocolate, if you'd like to join me."

That sounded all kinds of delicious… and routine. "Thank you." A little part of her stayed apprehensive, so she took a seat in the easy chair across from the love seat.

If Granger was disappointed, he didn't show it but nudged the steaming mug across the coffee table between them.

Pam blew across the top of hers as she inhaled the sweet fragrance.

"I made dinner at Melissa's tonight," Granger said conversationally. "Oliver didn't know that macaroni and cheese could be created without a box."

That had always been Roderick's favorite, too. Pam's had never competed, so she'd stopped trying. She'd saved her creativity for people who appreciated it.

Granger chuckled. "Sidney prefers the box, she said, but Ollie seemed to like my version. He sure had a good time here yesterday. The gingerbread house even made it into his school journal."

"Is it still upright?"

"Sort of? If the Leaning Tower of Pisa is considered upright."

Pam couldn't help the chuckle as her shoulders relaxed a tiny bit more. Why had she doubted Granger? He'd given no reason for her to believe he was a flight risk. "I'm glad you had a good visit with them."

"Me, too. Melissa asked about you."

So much for sitting easier. "Oh?"

"We have her blessing, in case it matters."

Tears sprang unbidden to Pam's eyes. It seemed the emotionally charged day wasn't giving up without a fight. "That's nice." What else could she say? She didn't know exactly what he meant. It sounded like Melissa thought her dad should marry Pam, but they were nowhere near that point. And could Pam really open herself up to those two children who reminded her so much of Courtney and Roderick? If she and Granger were truly an item, she'd have to.

No wonder she'd been downplaying whatever their relationship was. It wasn't only that she was too much, wasn't only that she didn't deserve a man like Granger, but those kids. What would Melissa think if she knew what a poor mother Pam had been? How focused on work she'd been to the detriment of her family?

"I've decided to buy a house here."

Pam refocused on the man seated across from her. "You have?"

"Melissa approves, and I don't have any real reason to return to Pennsylvania. I don't have a lot of close friends there. More like work colleagues. Jewel Lake is quickly becoming the home I've always wanted."

Pam had had a home, but what good did a shell do without someone to share it with? She'd sold their suburban house and most of its contents then moved into a condo without all the memories. But she'd scarcely been home even then.

"Creekside Fellowship is also the church home I've longed for. I'm so thankful for Marshall's and Eli's teaching and the opportunity to serve. I guess I could have gotten more involved in the congregation in Carlisle, but I didn't."

"This seems a good church," Pam ventured.

"It was a provocative sermon this morning."

Was he watching her for a reaction? "I wasn't feeling well, so I missed most of it." That wasn't exactly a lie. She'd managed to convince Loretta Satterfield that she didn't need an intervention before disappearing into the park beside the church. She'd found a well-worn path along the creek. She'd sat on a log for a while amid the fallen leaves and barren trees, feeling sorry for herself, but it had been chilly, and she wasn't dressed for it.

"I'm sorry to hear that. Are you... feeling better now?"

"Sort of." She let out a long breath. "It's an emotional thing. I'll get over it." But would she? Weren't post-menopausal women supposed to be over such powerful hormonal swings?

"Emotions are real." Granger's voice was so quiet she barely heard him.

Somehow his words gave her courage. "That song about praising the Lord... I had a sudden sense of overwhelm. Those words... 'Have you not seen all that is needful has been sent by His gracious ordaining?' I couldn't sit there and sing that."

"Because it feels like saying God purposed to take your husband and children from you?"

"Yes," she whispered.

"I don't think that's how it works."

That's how it felt it worked. That's what the song said, and weren't hymns like scripture, straight from the heart of God? Gospel truth in metered poetry, put to music. Pam took a shuddering breath. "I've always struggled with the sovereignty of God. There's so much trouble in the world. I know some people have it way worse than I did." Wendy, perhaps. "But is God in control, or isn't He? Either way, it doesn't seem like He's doing such a great job."

And now Granger knew the depths of her unbelief. If he needed an excuse to walk away from her, she'd handed it to him on a silver platter. Though he was buying a house in Jewel Lake, so it would be Pam who actually left.

So be it.

Granger shot a prayer heavenward. For Pam. For himself. It seemed everything hung in the balance. He needed God's wisdom. "The world is a mess. That's for sure."

She took a sip of her hot chocolate — probably lukewarm by now — and eyed him over the top of the mug.

"We don't understand God. If we could do that, He wouldn't be so different from us. All we know is that He created the universe, our world, and us. He loves us. He wants a relationship with us."

"Why? We're so weak and... and *silly*."

Was that how Pam thought of herself? She was the strongest woman he knew, and the farthest thing from foolish. But how to counter her words without brushing her off? He didn't do relationships with women for reasons like this. Evading landmines in enemy territory was easier.

"I think He knew exactly what He was doing when He created us as fragile humans. He didn't want robots who had no choice but to follow programming."

Pam scoffed lightly. "It would have been a lot easier."

"You're not wrong." But it wasn't the entire answer, and they both knew it. At least, he thought she must. "We have self-determination. We can choose whether to follow or not. Whether to embrace truth or reject it."

"It sort of makes sense, but I want it to make absolute sense."

Hopefully it was safe to insert a chuckle here. "I get it. But as complex as human brains are, they're as simple as amoebas' compared to God's."

"It shouldn't be this hard." Her voice was a bare whisper.

"He gives us every opportunity to lean on Him."

"By making life bone-crushingly difficult?"

She thought her life was the depths of despair? She'd never seen the starving, desperate children in war-torn parts of the world. Iraq would forever haunt him. Somalia. Afghanistan.

Pam set the mug down. "It's hard to give thanks in all things.

Am I really supposed to say 'thank You, God,' for taking my children before their time?"

Granger's heart crushed. "There are no platitudes for that situation."

"You think?" Her voice was bitter.

But wasn't trust still necessary? How did one keep moving forward when they stopped believing in the goodness of God? And that was a warning bell on its own. Had Pam rejected her faith? If so, he couldn't proceed in wooing her. That was not only the pathway to heartache for both of them, but disobedient. If Granger had learned anything in his Army years, it was that he needed to cling to God and not allow doubts to grab a foothold.

But was that blindness in its own right? Shouldn't a man be able to doubt and have his faith strengthened when God met him there? Because God would. Granger was one-hundred-percent certain of that. God had never failed him.

God hadn't failed Pam, either, no matter how she felt at the moment. God was there, desiring her renewed, deepened faith.

She pulled to her feet. "I should try to get some sleep."

Granger rose and stepped around the coffee table to intercept her. He opened his arms wide, and she stepped into them, resting her cheek against his chest. Even when he kissed her hair, she didn't lift her face to his. After a moment of cradling her against himself, he let his arms slacken.

Pam stepped back and offered a fleeting smile. "Thanks for the hot chocolate." Then she pivoted and strode to the elevator.

He waited until the doors slid closed behind her before sinking back into his seat. He rested his elbows on his knees as he leaned forward, roughing his hair with his hands. "God?" he whispered. "Is this already the end? I thought You had something planned for us."

Maybe it had all been wishful thinking on his part. Let the man escape from the confines of his career and the familiarities of his abode, and the first thing he does is try to fall in love.

Granger shook his head. That wasn't what had happened. He

hadn't been looking, but Pam had caught his attention from their very first meeting. She'd been so uptight. His grandkids had been so horrid. But God had given them another chance with both of them staying at Maranatha. Granger had seen past her facade and noticed a beautiful, talented, hurting woman.

Why did he feel the need to anchor her?

He couldn't. That was God's job.

Granger hated that. He was decisive. He was a fixer. In the Army, a soldier who wanted to stay alive didn't have the luxury of choice. Yes, he'd had to follow orders, but there wasn't a lot of room for wishy-washiness. For emotional setbacks. He'd soldiered on. Literally.

Pam might be struggling with the goodness of God, but Granger had his own battles. If he could whisk his magic wand and remove Pam's concerns, he'd do that in a heartbeat. He'd do it if it cost him his life.

But that wasn't what it would take. Pam had already mourned a husband and two children. Another loss wouldn't renew her faith.

What could Granger *do*? He couldn't sit back and fold his hands in defeat. That wasn't his way. And yet, the battle waged inside her, not anything he could sway. It wasn't his right, even if it were possible.

He could pray. Trust. Stand steadfastly beside her for as long as it took… unless she turned away completely.

Not an acceptable outcome.

Groaning, Granger tugged at his hair. It wasn't his battle. It was between God and Pam, and nothing made a man feel more helpless than standing aside while the woman he loved battled for her spiritual life.

Loved.

As little as a man with his history could understand of love, this was it.

He loved Pam.

CHAPTER
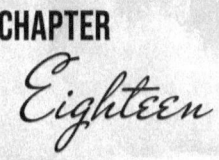
Eighteen

A m I interrupting you?"

Pam glanced up as Julia flopped dramatically into the chair across from her in the dining room. "I'm not doing anything too vital. I was just going over the supply order for Monday before I hit send. It can wait a few minutes."

"That was a great workshop." Julia waved her hand around the space where Wendy and Laura were still sweeping up cedar needles and straightening chairs.

"It was. Wendy's doing a terrific job. How many people registered for the event? Forty?"

"Forty-three, but a few couldn't make it."

"I noticed Monte was here." Pam couldn't resist poking at Julia.

"I'm glad men feel free to attend. It's not just women who want to celebrate Christmas with seasonal decor."

"Or maybe he was here for you."

Julia waved a hand. "We're just friends. I'm not sure why all of you persist in seeing something that doesn't exist."

"Oh, it exists, all right."

"I could ask you about Granger."

"You could, and I'd admit something exists, but I'm not sure it's going anywhere."

"Why ever not? He seems quite amazing, and he's certainly enthralled with you."

"One of these days he'll figure out I'm not as amazing as he deserves, and then we'll be history." It had been an awkward week. They'd gone to dinner and an action flick in Missoula on Tuesday night and chatted briefly by the fireside on evenings Pam worked, but the conversations had been superficial. Pam had made sure they didn't get too deep.

"You are absolutely amazing enough for a man like Granger Durand."

Pam shook her head. "Is that what's keeping you from dating Monte? I think if you gave him the slightest hint you'd accept, he'd be all over it."

"I don't know how to make you understand it's not like that."

One of these days, Julia would wake up and smell the roses. George had been a loving, attentive husband... but hadn't Mark looked like that to outsiders, too? Hmm. Somehow, Pam doubted anyone had been fooled. He'd been somewhat aloof with her friends on the rare occasions they'd all been together. Smiles hadn't reached his eyes, and he'd always excused himself to take a business call or the like. George, on the other hand, had seemed genuinely interested in anyone or anything Julia was into. Must've been nice.

"Granger mentioned he's been looking at real estate." Julia leaned closer across the table. "Are you going with him?"

"Of course not!"

"You're not the least bit curious about the Jewel Lake housing market and what he might find?"

Pam opened her mouth to deny it, but that would be lying, and wouldn't fool Julia for a second. "It's his decision. I'm just glad his daughter is happy to have him here."

"And you? It's not my desire to pressure you, but I do need to know soon if you're planning to stay at Maranatha or return to Charleston. It takes time to find a high-caliber chef."

"I know. I'm sorry. I just… I'm not quite sure yet."

"Is it because of Granger? Because that man looks at you like you hung the moon. If you give him any encouragement at all, you'll be wearing a diamond in no time."

"One word."

Julia smiled expectantly, her eyes dancing. "Yes?"

"Monte."

"What?" She looked confused.

"I don't think you qualify to give me relationship advice when you're playing ostrich with your head stuck in the sand."

Julia sighed. "It's not that. It's… George. Sometimes it feels like he's gone on a business trip and he'll come in the front door anytime, look around, whistle appreciatively, and tell me I did an amazing job getting the inn running in his absence, but he's back now to take his place at my side."

"He's gone, hon." Pam gentled her voice as much as she could. "He's not coming in the door."

"I know that. I do, but somehow it still seems so unfinished with him. I miss him so much, Pammy."

"I'm sorry." Pam reached across the table and covered Julia's hand.

"Me, too. I like having a good plan, and I love when it comes together. You and I are alike that way."

Pam nodded.

"And George dying before we even broke ground for the inn was *not* in the plan. It just wasn't."

"I get it. The accident that took Mark and the kids was definitely not in my plan, either."

Julia turned her hand over and gripped Pam's. "Are you doing okay? I know it's been a lot of years, but it seems like grief has a way of resurfacing when one least expects it."

"That's the truth." Not that Pam wanted to reveal more. She'd already admitted enough to Granger. More than enough. "I'm mostly okay."

"Is it easier or harder being here so far from everything you and Mark shared?"

Pam pondered. "I'm not sure. I'm not really looking forward to a Montana winter, but there are good things, too."

"Are you…" Julia bit her lip. "I know I shouldn't pressure you, but are you truly thinking of staying?"

"I'm considering it." Pam held up a hand. "But I'm not sure. I know you need to know soon."

"I was hoping with Granger…"

"You shouldn't hope." Never, not even in the quietest recesses of one's brain.

"Okay." Julia sighed. "If we wind up needing to close the restaurant for a few weeks in January due to not having a chef, it's not the end of the world. We do have a week-long booking for a skiing group, but they can probably take their dinners in town."

Way to load on the guilt. And yet, Pam was leaving things open-ended, and Julia would bear the brunt. "I'll try to have a definitive answer for you within a week."

"That would be super helpful. And… Pam?" Julia waited until their gazes met. "I want you to do what's best for you. What God wants *you* to do. Don't worry about me, or about Maranatha Inn. If it's God's plan for you to leave us, then He has something else in store for us here."

Just like that? Pam's eyebrows tipped up.

"I'm hoping and praying you'll stay, though. It's been so good to have the gang together, and I think everyone's getting along well now."

If by that, Julia meant that Audrey had stopped sniping at Wendy about her weight, maybe. At least, her disapproval wasn't quite as vocal as it had been the first couple of weeks. "Things seem to be smoother."

"I can always count on you. You're so level-headed, and you're so kind and understanding with everyone."

Pam made a show of looking over first one shoulder then the other. "Who are you talking to?"

"You, silly. No theatrics."

"Then I guess you don't know me very well. Inside my head? Constant drama." Hopefully, she'd kept her voice light enough that Julia wouldn't quite catch just how much Pam locked inside each and every day.

Granger looked around the tidy two-bedroom townhome. How much better could it be than two blocks from Melissa's? He wasn't into a ton of yard work and, if he wanted to indulge, he doubted his daughter would mind if he did it at her place.

"What do you think?" the agent asked. "It's a brand-new listing, and I don't think it will last long at this price point."

Typical sales push, but Granger had been eyeing the market for a few weeks, unsure if he'd be jumping in or not. Very few houses sold this time of year but, on the other hand, this listing was recent. "Why are they selling in November? Job transfer?"

"No, the elderly woman has been admitted to a long-term care home, and her family has decided to liquidate the assets."

"So it's ready for occupancy?" Granger had been surprised to find a furnished house but with no personal touches.

"They decided to leave the furniture for now. If the buyer wants them included, great. If not, the family will remove them at that time."

Granger's place in Pennsylvania had come furnished, and he wasn't attached to any of it. That left a few boxes of personal items he could get his friend to ship. He might not even need to return.

He looked around the place thoughtfully. He'd want to replace some of the items — that floral easy chair was a bit much — but he could do so at his leisure. "I'd like to bring my daughter by tomorrow. If she's in favor, I'll put in an offer then."

"Will she be living with you?" The agent's eyebrows rose.

"No. She and her children live a couple of blocks up the hill. But I still value a woman's input."

"There's no Mrs. Durand?"

Not that it was any of the agent's business. "No." And Granger wasn't sure if he should invite Pam to see the house before closing, either. It had been an odd week, like waiting for the other boot to fall. He honestly didn't know if there was going to be a future with her. Trying to hold the situation in an open palm before the Lord was hard.

The agent consulted his phone. "We could do the same time tomorrow, if that's an option for you."

"My daughter works until five. Are you available after that?"

"Five fifteen?"

"Sure. We can do that."

"These are solid units in this complex. There's even a play-ground in the middle for your grandchildren. I don't think you'll regret purchasing here."

"Sounds good." Granger stuck out his hand. "Tomorrow, then?"

The agent drove away, leaving Granger sitting in his car at the curb. Could he see himself living here? It was all one level, perfect for aging. Not that he liked thinking about becoming old and decrepit, but he also didn't want to move again for a long, long time. Maybe like the current owner, heading into a nursing home.

Granger grimaced. He'd rather die in a war zone than have life seep away little by little. Mostly, a man didn't get to choose.

He shoved the thought of his eventual demise out of his head. Could this house be a home? His home?

If Pam were in it.

He could envision them cooking together in the compact, yet adequate, kitchen. He could see them savoring a drink on the patio out back before she headed for a shift at the inn. He could see them curled up on that love seat by the fireplace on her evenings off. Hey, he'd even keep the floral armchair if she liked it.

Would she be open to seeing the house? Being part of the decision? Or would that be enough pressure to send her fleeing for South Carolina?

He didn't know. It had been such a weird week. They'd kept their habit of lingering by the fireside after she closed the kitchen, but any kissing had been perfunctory. Their discussions had been surface. How were plans coming for the church outreach event? Had he found a Santa suit to wear? Were any of the new guests at the inn staying more than one or two nights? Wasn't the weather lovely for mid-November?

Nothing that mattered.

Granger growled in frustration. He was used to action, not waffling. Definitely not pretending nothing was wrong when something obviously was. Was he simply too chicken to confront Pam on the topic? What if she turned out to be a weepy woman? He couldn't abide that. He also couldn't see it. Not put-together Pam. She was the epitome of self-control.

Could there be too much willpower? He stared at the townhouse until it blurred. The question persisted. Was a little emotion better than excessive constraint?

If their kisses this week were any indication, yes. A marriage required emotion.

Whoa, Durand. Back up a bit. Who's talking wedding bells?

He'd be 60 years old in a few weeks. Some would say he'd been alone this long, and he'd be better off sticking it out. On the other hand, why waste time playing games when he'd found the woman he wanted to spend the rest of his life with?

So, yeah, the wedding bells chimed in his mind, but caution was still necessary. This wasn't a military mission: in and out with as many casualties as possible to the enemy, while sustaining the lowest possible amount of damage to his side.

Relationships required give and take. Understanding. Nuance.

Granger was not good at those things. What had made him an excellent leader and, eventually, a colonel, were not the skills he needed to make a relationship with Pam work.

He wasn't even certain she had the same goals he did. Right now, he wasn't willing to rock the boat to find out. If she ultimately decided to return to Charleston, he'd prefer to live in his little hopeful bubble a bit longer.

CHAPTER
Nineteen

T think that's it." Pam scanned her list one more time. Every item had been struck through, but had she remembered to note everything on it in the first place?

Granger and Eli stood beside the island in the inn's kitchen.

Eli reached for a box. "You're so organized. Now it's our job to deliver these boxes to our volunteer cooks."

"Please. Laura taped the names and addresses and instructions to each box." Pam bit her lip. "I do hope I haven't forgotten anything." How could she have? She'd combed every recipe for every ingredient. She and Julia and Wendy had loaded each box with care while Laura printed out the directions to include.

"May we use the luggage trolley to take these out to the trucks?" Granger asked Julia.

"Of course!"

"I'll grab it for you," Laura offered, already pivoting out of the space. She was back in a minute with the trolley, which the men loaded in record time.

Pam felt Granger's eyes on her several times, but she stayed focused on her master list. Not that there was anything left to check.

"We've got this now. You ladies make time for a cup of tea." Granger gave the trolley a nudge, and Eli took it from there.

Pam laughed. "Now that I have my kitchen back, it's time to start prepping for tonight's dinner."

Julia slid her arm around Pam's waist. "We can take ten."

Pam stifled her protest. Whose job was it to make sure tonight's guests were wowed? Satisfied wasn't enough. Pam wanted — needed — them to tell everyone how amazing the food was. How lovely the inn. How attentive the staff. How their expectations had been exceeded.

Maybe she took too much on herself. Some of that was Julia's jurisdiction, and some the wait staff's.

But the meal was still Pam's responsibility.

The doors swished shut behind the men. Julia stood at the sink, filling the kettle for tea.

Wendy came out of the pantry with a container of pumpkin chocolate chip muffins. "These are leftovers, right?"

"Um, yes, we could have those if Jilly didn't mark them otherwise."

"No note on them."

"Perfect. I guess I've been outvoted. Break time it is."

Laura steered her to a table and gently pushed her into a chair. "You're amazing, Pam. Do you know that?"

Pam blinked back tears. "No, I don't know that."

"Well, let me count the ways." Wendy laid the container on the table. "I can't imagine all the moving parts in planning a meal like this for other people to cook."

"You're pretty amazing yourself, Wendy." Julia set a tray with teacups on the table and handed them out. "The events you've planned and hosted are all I'd hoped for."

"Really?" Wendy scooped sugar into her tea.

At least Audrey wasn't in the room to make a comment or roll her eyes. She'd had a fitness session planned for this afternoon with some of the inn's guests, so she'd bowed out of helping with the meals.

"Julia's right," Laura said. "Not to take away from Pam's excellent oversight of the meal, but don't undercut yourself, Wendy. You planned the rest of the outreach event—"

"With Granger."

"Yes, with Granger, but you pulled it together. If it's anything like our Saturday workshops here, it will be amazing."

Pam could only be glad they'd shifted the focus from her. It was good to see Wendy glow from their friends' praise. Besides, she had Beef Wellingtons to prepare shortly. The mushrooms were already chopped for the duxelles, so it was just a matter of—

"Pam?"

"Sorry?" She turned to Julia.

"Do you need extra help with the inn's Thanksgiving dinner tomorrow? I should have thought to ask you earlier."

Pam mentally turned the page in her planner from Wednesday — where her mind had gone after dealing with Saturday — to Thursday. They'd thought to limit reservations for the traditional turkey meal, assuming most people would prefer to enjoy the holiday with their families. Still, nearly 50 plates had been ordered with a single sit-down time of 6pm. The Satterfields were in town again and bringing their daughter and son-in-law, Harper and Eli Bryson, to dinner. Granger had invited Melissa and the children... and asked Pam if she'd like to join them. She'd put off answering.

Wendy's two unmarried daughters were due to arrive late tonight.

Monte, on the other hand, had bowed out, citing a tradition with Sheryl's family. This was his sister and brother-in-law's first Thanksgiving together since remarrying a few months ago, so it was a big deal.

Pam turned to Julia. "No, I think we're good. Mostly because you insisted we'd serve cafeteria style at a single seating."

"Because I wanted you to enjoy dinner along with everyone else. It wouldn't be fair if you were slaving away while the rest of us relaxed."

"It's what you pay me the big bucks for."

Laura snickered, and Wendy laughed outright, but Pam knew for a fact that her wage was higher than either of theirs. As it should be... but maybe 'big bucks' was a slight exaggeration.

"Well, Wendy and I will make sure the dining room is ready." Julia beamed. "Those centerpieces Wendy made are beautiful."

Pam hadn't even seen them. She'd been neck-deep in planning food for the outreach event.

"I'll help in the kitchen if you can use an extra set of hands," Laura put in. "Or at least help clear tables and run the dishwasher."

"I'm sure we can count on Audrey and Chris, too," Julia went on. "We'll all be hostesses for the evening."

"Then I can't ask for anything more." Even with an offer of double pay, Darla had requested the evening off, but Pam wasn't worried. Darla would do a lot of the prep in slower times tonight and, with the other women's help, tomorrow would run smoothly enough. It was a gathering of friends, after all.

Friends plus Granger's grandchildren.

Pam released a slow breath. She needed to decide whether to join them or feign busyness, but she couldn't put it off forever. Not unless she decided Granger wasn't worth the effort. It wasn't that. He was definitely worth it.

It was her. *She* wasn't worth his time, though he didn't see it that way.

Could she take the risk? She'd thought she'd put everything on the line already, agreeing to headline Maranatha Inn's dining experience for three months. But she hadn't counted on meeting someone who tempted her to change her entire life.

She hadn't counted on falling in love.

"Well, that's the last of them." Eli closed the tailgate then dusted his hands together. "I can't thank you enough for all the work you've done pulling this event together. When I talked to Marshall about it last month, I basically admitted that it was too much to deal with and that it wouldn't happen."

"I'm glad to help, but without the women at Maranatha, I know I couldn't have pulled it off, either. Especially not a meal on this grand of a scale."

Eli shook his head, grinning. "It looks perfect. At least, if the volunteers follow instructions well. It's out of Pam's hands now. And into God's."

Granger chuckled. "I don't think Pam has quite let go. She'll be on pins and needles until after everything has been cleaned up on Saturday."

"I understand that, actually. Let me drop you back to the inn, and I'll head over to the office to wrap up a few things. Short workweeks always mess with me."

"I should have brought my own car and saved you the trouble."

"It's no problem. Maranatha isn't that far out of town. Not like Rockstead or Sweet River."

Granger hopped into the passenger seat as Eli started the truck. Soon they were turning off the road past the Happy Trails Stables sign.

Eli gestured toward it. "Been for a horseback ride yet?"

"No, I haven't stopped in. I did meet the owners at the ginger-bread house event a couple of weeks ago, though. They seem like lovely young women."

"They are. We've put in a few miles of riding trails over the summer and fall."

"We?" Granger angled toward the young pastor.

"Yep. I've done a lot of volunteering with the Jewel Lake Trails Society over the past decade or so, so I had the experience and connections to point the girls in the right direction. We had a good-sized crew from the town, so it went smoothly."

"Huh. I never thought about what something like that might entail."

"You should take your grandkids riding there sometime."

"I never thought of that, but you're right." Would Sidney be intrigued, or would she turn up her nose at the idea? The only way to know would be to ask. Maybe once the outreach event was over, he could focus on other things. Like hiring cleaners for the house he'd just bought and could take possession of at the end of November.

Like Pam, because he couldn't let this uneasy situation continue indefinitely. But they did have a few events to get through before either of them could focus on their relationship... which hopefully they'd still have afterward. And that fear kept him from tackling the subject now. If there wasn't going to be a 'them,' he wasn't ready to face it yet.

Eli rounded the circular drive and parked in front of the inn, which gleamed white against the evergreens behind it. A couple of late, deep red roses bloomed in the sheltered spot beside the front door, vying for attention with the nearby Christmas wreaths.

"It's hard to believe this place is in Jewel Lake," Eli commented. "It always feels like I've stepped into some upscale urban environment when I arrive here."

Granger chuckled. "I know what you mean. And yet, somehow, it seems to suit its surroundings."

"Julia made sure of that. She's worked hard to fit into the community, like delivering complimentary lunches to Happy Trails on the community workdays there."

"She did that?"

Eli nodded. "And it was before her chef arrived, so it was all her and Chris. She built a lot of goodwill with that generosity."

"Wow. I didn't know. She seems like quite the woman."

"She really is." Eli grinned. "But I think someone else got to her first."

"What?" Granger burst out laughing. "Oh, you mean Monte

Newman. I hear they're just friends, but that's their problem, not mine. I'm far more interested in Pamela Whorley."

"I'd heard rumors from my in-laws."

"Vance and Loretta? Yeah, they seem to stay at the inn a lot, and they're interested in everything and everyone."

"They're amazing people, but I promise you'll see much less of them over the winter. They're southerners who are convinced the slightest skiff of snow — never mind the sight of their breath in the cold air! — is the epitome of winter, and they've now survived a full-on blizzard."

"That's hilarious."

"But it's still true. If Marshall's health wasn't suffering, and I wasn't so busy with the church, they'd insist Harper and I visit Atlanta more often. But they respect that I can't get away as easily as they can, so they visit us here. They love staying at Maranatha Inn, so that helps but, trust me, they'll be scarce between Christmas and Easter."

"Vance seems like an insightful man."

"He is. I couldn't have asked for better in-laws. Truly."

Granger had heard Eli's story of being brought up in foster care, so he understood how much it meant to have this accepting relationship. "Well, I should let you get back to the office."

Eli checked his watch. "Right. See you tomorrow."

Granger exited the truck and waited until Eli drove away before entering the inn. The place was just as stunning on the inside as it was on the outside. Thanksgiving might be tomorrow, but Julia was in full Christmas mode. There'd been one enormous decorated tree even when Granger arrived in late September, but lights and decorations and festive throw cushions had multiplied in the public spaces over the intervening weeks.

He sniffed appreciatively of cinnamon and cranberries as Julia looked up from the front desk. "Get all the food delivered?"

"We did. It's out of our hands now."

She smiled. "The cooks will do a great job."

"I'm sure. I'm still nervous about the whole thing on Saturday, though."

"Don't be. You and Pam make a great team." Her eyes twinkled. "Oh, and Wendy."

"Laura, too." Granger didn't want to dwell on him and Pam. "She's got an amazing voice, and I'm glad she's singing for the program."

"And you have people coming for the trees on Friday morning?"

He nodded. "Twelve businesses signed up to decorate trees and donate them. It should be pretty cool."

"Twelve families will be very happy."

"I hope so." He hesitated. "I got a tree for Melissa already, so she won't put her name in. She has a job, unlike some of our guests that night."

"Bless you, Granger. You're a fine man."

His cheeks flushed. "Thank you. I'm trying to look after my family after years of... not."

"All we can do about the past is acknowledge it, learn our lessons, thank God for forgiveness, and face forward."

"That is so true. I've been guilty of kicking myself in the rear over my past failures, but it doesn't help."

"It really doesn't. In fact, it can paralyze any forward motion."

Movement across the dining hall caught Granger's attention, and he looked over to see Pam disappearing into the kitchen.

He could only hope that she didn't take his words as criticizing her coping methods.

CHAPTER

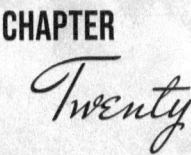

They made it sound like turning things over to God was easy. Ha! If it were so simple, she would have accomplished it years ago.

Pam shoved the memory of the overheard conversation into a compartment in the back of her brain and locked it. She'd become good at this. Cooking at the level she'd achieved required absolute focus.

Mark slid his arms around her from behind and nuzzled her neck. She laughed and turned toward him. A few minutes later, the smoke alarm screeched.

Dinner had been ruined by her inattention. They'd ordered in pizza.

Distractions had never been allowed since.

At the end of her shift, she passed Granger where he rose by the fireplace. "I'm too tired tonight." Truth lay in that statement. The hours had been long between finalizing all the boxes and then cooking dinner in the restaurant.

"I'm sorry, but I understand."

And she fled. She didn't deserve a man like him. He'd overcome his past regrets to make things right with his daughter. No similar option existed for Pam. Her family was irrevocably gone. Her failure couldn't be reversed.

Pam couldn't settle enough to even pretend to sleep. Her mind threatened to explode. Her staff suite wasn't big enough for pacing. She didn't want to sit with scripture. Finally, she donned her swimsuit and tiptoed out to the hot tub. Maybe she could unwind here. She needed sleep to get through Thanksgiving dinner and the days following. Today had only been the beginning of a crazy busy workweek.

Lights sprang on in the staff lounge just inside, and Pam turned away from the brightness, sinking deeper into the churning hot water. Maybe she could remain unnoticed. Chatting with any of her friends was the last thing she wanted.

The French doors opened, and Wendy spoke. "Just wait until you see this in daylight! We've got a private patio and hot tub here for the staff, and... Pam? Is that you?"

How could Pam have forgotten Wendy's girls would arrive tonight? The only thing worse than being discovered out here by one of her friends was the addition of even more people. Too late now.

She waved. "Hi! Yes, it's me, just unwinding before bed. It's been a busy day." And an emotionally draining week, not that she was ready to spill all that.

"Girls, you remember Aunt Pam, right? Pam, Selah and Faith are here for the weekend!"

"Welcome to Montana!"

"It's good to be here. Mom's talked so much about this place."

That had been the older girl, right? Pam couldn't see them clearly, silhouetted against the bright light as they were. "You'll have to get the grand tour in the morning."

"Oh, we will!"

"See you tomorrow, Pammy!" The widest of the three silhouettes turned back inside, and the others followed.

A few seconds later, the lights dimmed as the trio made their way to Wendy's suite. Wendy had claimed two cots from the storage room for her daughters for the weekend.

Pam turned back to the dark night.

Courtney had been about the same age as Selah. She would never come for a visit.

How was Pam supposed to learn her lesson from that? She hadn't caused the accident. An inexperienced semi-truck driver had rolled his load and crushed Mark's car. Her family hadn't stood a chance.

It wasn't her fault.

She knew that. There was nothing to acknowledge there.

Then why did guilt remain?

False guilt, she'd been told.

Pam hadn't returned to the counselor's office. No point. She'd muddled through on her own. Sometimes, she'd even done a decent job, or so she'd thought. Now? Evidence indicated otherwise.

And we know that for those who love God all things work together for good, for those who are called according to his purpose.

Romans 8:28 only proved she didn't love God, that she wasn't called according to His purpose, because things had not worked together for good. Simple.

She squeezed her eyes tight, trying to stem the burning tears. Problem? She did love God or, at least, she thought she did. But the sense of failure refused to recede, no matter how many culinary accolades she'd earned. They remained hollow when there was no one with whom to give and receive love.

Today, the whole team had carried out her plans and praised her for them. Granger. Eli. Julia. Wendy. Laura.

She hadn't felt so included, so much a part of something solid and good, since long before she and Mark had separated all those years ago.

Granger might even love her.

She might love him back.

But the price seemed too high. The chasm too wide.

She wasn't the person he thought she was.

Satan is a liar.

Pam's eyes sprang open. Who'd said that? No one sat in the hot tub with her. Her eyes scanned beyond the patio where a few solar lights dotted the fall landscape. The hillside beyond was black in the night, silhouetted against a crisp, starry sky.

Silence was absolute.

No one was outside with her.

God had promised never to leave her or forsake her. She might fool other people into thinking she was worth sticking around for, but God saw through her smoke and mirrors and knew the real her. He loved her anyway.

Satan is a liar.

Had she been listening to the wrong voice? Because this one sounded true. Felt true. Satan had every interest in sabotaging her. In subverting all of God's creation. He wanted to lure all who'd been created in God's image, every single person, into believing lies.

What kinds of lies?

Lies of worthlessness.

Because those cut the knees out from everyone who listened, tumbling them to the ground, unable to stand. Failures.

There was nothing for her back in Charleston. Nothing but work. Sure, she had several top restaurants clamoring for her to join their staff, but they didn't care about her, just about what she could do for their bottom line.

Julia cared about her at a much deeper level. And what would happen to her friends here if she left? Who would keep Audrey from sniping at Wendy? Who would draw Chris out? Who would gentle Laura's drama?

Who would love Granger?

Did she have a purpose after all? Were things finally working out for good?

Did that mean she needed to give thanks for her family's deaths? It wasn't even possible.

Granger's phone chimed, and he reached for it, stilling when he saw that Pam had texted. After last night's evasion, how could he summon the courage to read her words? But he needed to.

Pam: *Is the offer still on to have dinner with your family tonight?*

He blinked. Not at all what he'd expected or braced himself for.

Granger: *Always. I can't wait!*

He checked the time. She'd be in the kitchen already, working away on what should be a holiday. But, hey, didn't couples all across the USA cook holiday dinners together? Maybe they were a couple after all.

It only took five minutes for him to make his way to the doorway of the inn's kitchen, where he paused until she looked up. Laura and Julia were in there with her. Good, but not enough. "Can I help?"

Pam hesitated, but Laura waved him in. "The more the merrier. Wash up over there, and you can peel potatoes."

"Sure, unless the boss has a better idea." He might be answering Laura, but his gaze remained fixed on Pam. She gave him a small smile. He'd take that as a welcome as he crossed to the handwashing station beside the restroom door, where he scrubbed up like a surgeon headed into the operating room. Then he paused beside Pam and nudged her shoulder with his arm. "What's the game plan?"

She leaned slightly against him.

He'd take it.

"It's lovely having several large ovens. The turkeys and hams are roasting."

Granger sniffed the air. "And smell amazing."

Pam smiled. "The roasted vegetables are almost ready to go in. Julia is finishing those up as we speak."

Julia waved her chef's knife from the large butcher block counter. "Ready in ten."

"Darla prepped the salads yesterday and made the desserts." Pam eyed Julia's back. "Too bad Monte couldn't make it today, or I'd have asked him to bring pies. That man bakes a mean dessert."

Julia laughed but didn't turn. "I've probably gained five pounds in the past year because he keeps dropping food by."

Granger chuckled. He'd been the recipient of more than one mouth-watering pastry from Monte's kitchen himself.

"Laura's on potatoes." Pam raised her eyebrows at her friend.

"Until Granger arrived." Laura gave him an exaggerated wink. "Now I'm going to go set tables. Wendy and her girls should be up any minute to help with that."

"They arrived last night?"

Pam pulled away from him. "They did."

What was all that about? Not like he'd ask. For now, it was enough that Pam had reached out to him. He peered over her shoulder. "What are you making?"

"Sweet potato casseroles."

"Yum."

"You like those?"

"I grew up in Georgia. 'Nuff said."

"We've got quite a mix of backgrounds signed up for dinner tonight."

Julia turned toward them. "Stop worrying about it, Pam. We're the hosts. They're our guests, not our bosses."

"Right."

Granger nudged Pam again, careful to keep his hands airborne since he'd just washed. "What she said."

"Thanks."

"These potatoes aren't going to peel themselves," Laura called.

He laughed and reached for her paring knife. "Get out of here."

"I should remind you you're a guest," Julia commented.

"Noted. Not that it will stop me." He picked up a potato and began peeling it.

She chuckled. "You've been warned."

Peppy praise music filtered from the speakers in the ceiling but didn't quite cover the voices from the dining room. He'd known two of Wendy's daughters were coming for the weekend. Once again, he tried to imagine six children. Failed. Tried to imagine a man who would toss out the mother of his six children. Failed, this time with anger.

Wendy was a valuable child of God. Hopefully the time with her girls would be positive. Life-giving.

He could use these minutes to sing along with the songs in his head and to pray.

Julia slid several large pans of vegetables into an oven. "What's next?"

Nothing. Go away. I've got it. But Granger wouldn't say any of those things out loud.

"I think everything's covered until we need to start taking things out of ovens. Any volunteers for carving the meat?"

Julia held up both hands. "Preferably not me. That was always George's job."

"Granger?"

He grimaced. "Not if you care about them being perfect. I've never done it."

"Of course, I care."

Right. Ms. Everything-needs-to-be-perfect. But didn't that beat not caring? Likely a happy medium existed in there somewhere.

Julia dried her hands by the sink. "I'll ask Vance Satterfield. I bet he's a pro."

"Thanks." Pam slipped the casserole dish into the oven. "If not, I can do it. It's just that it lands right when everything else needs doing, too."

"I'll find you a carver." And Julia headed through the swinging doors.

Granger dropped the last peeled potato into the pot. "Is it time to start cooking these?"

Pam nodded. "It takes a while for that large pot to come to a boil. Mind lifting it over to the range?" She moved in that direction.

"No problem." He lifted the heavy thing and set it in place. "Do you haul those around on the regular?"

She shrugged. "I'm capable of it, but it is pretty heavy." She turned on the element.

"You can do anything you put your mind to, woman. You're amazing."

Her gaze flicked off his. "Not so much."

Granger stepped in front of her and reached for her hands. Finally, she looked up at him. "Don't listen to lies like that. I've seen you in action for six weeks now. You *are* amazing. It's not up for debate."

Pam blinked at him, and her mouth gaped for a few seconds before she snapped it shut. "How did you know?" she whispered.

He gentled his voice. "Know what?"

"That's exactly what God called me out on late last night. I heard His voice, clear as I can hear yours right now."

Oh, boy. Granger searched her eyes. "What did He say?"

"Satan is a liar."

Wow. "That's true."

"I know. I didn't realize I'd been listening. That I'd been absorbing those lies as truth."

A dozen questions tumbled through Granger's mind, but none of them seemed safe to ask. She'd tell him more if she wanted to, and maybe now wasn't the time.

The thought was confirmed when the kitchen doors swung open, and a young woman entered. "Aunt Pam? Mom said to ask you where the appetizer cups are."

"Selah. Good to see you, honey." Pam stepped away from Granger. "They're in this cupboard over here. I hope you and Faith had a good sleep on those cots."

"Not bad." The girl shrugged. "Seems weird for Mom to be so far from home, though."

How long ago had Wendy and her ex split up? Granger'd gotten the impression it had been a while, but Selah spoke like togetherness had been a more recent thing.

"We're all so happy your mom joined us here at Maranatha. I think it's been a good thing for her. I know it's been good for me to be here."

Granger's heart warmed.

The girl glanced between him and Pam. "What kind of good?"

"So many ways," Pam replied. "One of them has been meeting this man, Granger Durand. Granger, this is Wendy's daughter Selah."

"I'm pleased to meet you." He nodded at the young woman. "Your mom is really gifted at organization and planning events. It's a pleasure working with her here."

Selah's eyebrows rose. "Are we talking about *my* mother?"

"If you're Wendy Clarke's daughter."

"Huh. Thanks." She loaded a tray with cups and headed back out the door.

Granger watched Pam bite her lip as she stared after Selah.

Seemed like more than Wendy's ex doubted her abilities and worth.

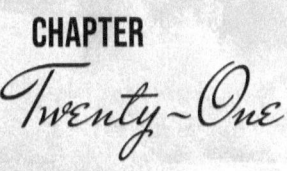

Twenty~One

P am stepped back and surveyed the heated buffet table, loaded with all the makings of a feast.

"Looks good, Pamela." Vance Satterfield stood beside her. The man had come through, expertly carving the turkeys while Granger had sliced the hams.

"It does." She lifted the ladle full of gravy and poured it back. It ran smooth as velvet. She took a deep breath. "I think we're ready to invite everyone into the dining room." Julia had offered to host simple appetizers and drinks in the lobby as their guests gathered.

Vance touched her arm. "You did well."

She met his gaze. "Thank you." She couldn't have said why this meal made her more nervous than usual. Okay, yes, she did. She'd agreed to join Granger's family and officially meet them as his girlfriend. Didn't a more sophisticated title exist for folks in their 50s? Significant other, maybe, but what a mouthful.

Pam released a long breath, crossed into the lobby, and caught Julia's eye. At Julia's raised eyebrows, Pam nodded.

Julia clapped her hands. "We are ready for dinner. Pastor Eli, could I ask you to give thanks for this feast?"

"Absolutely." Eli took his place beside Julia. "Father God, we come before you today with humble gratitude for the good things You have provided for us — good food and good friends. We are thankful for the hard times that draw us closer to You. And most of all, we are thankful for the gift of Your Son, who died that we might live. Please bless our fellowship tonight. In Jesus's name, amen."

"We'll form a line to load up our plates," Julia went on. "Then please find your name on a place card, as we have assigned seating this evening. Thank you for coming tonight, my friends." She gestured toward the buffet table.

Everyone looked at each other.

Julia laughed. "Wendy, why don't you and your girls go first? Next, Eli and Harper. Then everyone else. Please don't be shy."

Wendy's face flushed at being singled out, but she nudged her girls ahead of her and opened the line.

Pam fought the urge to stand behind the buffet table and make sure everything was perfect. Being a guest at her own dinner seemed counterintuitive, but that didn't keep her from being grateful for the compromise Julia had suggested.

Now... her gaze connected with Granger's. He smiled, seeming to sense her hesitation. This was hard.

She breathed a prayer and made her way around the throng to where he stood with his daughter and grandchildren.

Granger engulfed her left hand in his right one. "Pam, I'd like you to meet my daughter, Melissa. Melissa, this is Pam, tonight's chef and the woman who's captured my heart."

Pam didn't miss Sidney's eye roll as she shook Melissa's hand. "It's really good to meet you."

"Likewise." Melissa's eyes seemed clear and welcoming.

"Kids, this is my friend Pam. Pam, this is Sidney and Oliver."

Sidney raised her eyebrows. "She's the lady from the diner."

Pam managed to hold her smile in place. "Yes, we did see each other for the first time there."

Oliver elbowed his sister. "Why did you eat your sandwich with a fork and knife?"

Granger put his arm around the boy's shoulders. "It isn't any of your business."

The kid didn't forget anything. "It seemed too thick to take a bite out of otherwise. My mouth isn't that big."

Sidney opened hers, possibly to argue. Melissa touched her, and the girl subsided.

"I think we're next in line." Granger squeezed Pam's hand. "Shall we?"

Melissa and Sidney went first, and Pam looked up at Granger. "Thanks," she whispered.

"For?"

For what, indeed? Sticking up for her? Keeping a firm grip on her hand, which helped her keep a firm grip on her sanity? "For being you."

Granger released her hand only to slip his arm around her back, tugging her close to his side. "Back at you."

Sidney hadn't been outright hostile, right? Pam could earn the girl's trust, maybe even her friendship.

Not if Sidney ever found out how badly Pam had messed up her relationship with Courtney.

Satan is a liar.

Pam needed to cling to God's truth. She might not have been the best mom in the world, but she'd loved her kids. Courtney had been going through early puberty. Pam had been no dream child when she'd been that age, either.

She loaded up a plate at the buffet and followed Melissa and the children to their table set for eight. Wendy and her daughters had already taken their seats. Pam might have wished for different table companions, but why? She didn't fear Granger's attention straying to her friend.

Maybe it wasn't all about her. Maybe Wendy needed to sit near Pam, needed a friend who was definitely on her side.

Granger performed the introductions. Sidney eyed the older girls with interest. At 16, Faith might seem like a role model to a 12-year-old. In turn, Faith's attention was riveted to her 20-year-old sister.

Seemed like girls always needed someone to look up to. Pam had, too. She'd looked up to Mark. How had she expected him to guide her and validate her in every way? Even her culinary awards had meant little if he didn't tell her he was proud of her.

Hmm. She'd file that memory away to consider later.

"This is delicious." Melissa smiled at Pam. "So, you're the chief chef around here."

"Thank you, and yes."

"I like the sweet potatoes," Selah offered.

Oliver took a bite of his and wrinkled his nose. "I don't. They're yucky."

"Oliver," Melissa warned. "We don't say that."

"He's right, though." Sidney pushed hers to one side. "Are these Brussels sprouts? I don't like those, either."

Pam gritted her teeth. The meal had been planned to meet traditional expectations for adult palates. She couldn't help it if the kids didn't like it. Hadn't Granger said they preferred boxed macaroni and cheese? Kids had no tastebuds whatsoever.

"I like them." Faith popped one in her mouth.

"You do?" A puzzled expression crossed Sidney's face.

"Yeah, they're delish. Mom used to make them all the time. These are a little different, though. Your recipe, Aunt Pam?"

Wendy looked down and dragged her fork through her mashed potatoes.

"She's your aunt?" Oliver asked, eyes wide.

"Not really. But she and Mom have been friends forever, so we call her that."

"Isn't that like lying?"

Faith frowned. "Why would it be?"

Selah rolled her eyes. "It's more like an honorary title of respect." Her expression revealed she didn't think the Everett kids knew anything about respect.

She might not be wrong.

"So," Melissa interjected rather loudly, "you're the one who was in charge of the gingerbread house project, right, Wendy? Oliver sure enjoyed that day."

Good for Melissa trying to turn the conversation.

Granger felt like he'd never held his breath quite so much as he had over dinner. Landmines seemed to be popping up all over. His grandkids were not on their best behavior, and things between Wendy and her daughters seemed awkward at best. He couldn't do anything about any of that, but it wasn't how he'd envisioned the evening. He'd never wondered who else might be assigned to their table. No doubt it had made good sense to Julia to pair their five-some and Wendy's threesome together, when the two women were good friends.

In actuality? It was all kinds of awkward.

Bless her, Melissa did her best. Pam, too. Granger tried to put everyone at ease, but the edge remained.

"I'm thankful for everyone who could join us this evening." Julia's voice rang out from beside the buffet table. "There is more food for anyone who would like a second helping. Meanwhile, though, Laura is handing out papers to all the tables with icebreakers on them. Now, you may already know everyone at your table, but we think it will still be fun to play along. You may find yourself with new insights about your friends and companions!"

Laura moved between the tables, distributing printouts.

Granger couldn't help wondering if the topic would be helpful or not so much. He thanked Laura for the sheet and scanned it before looking around the table. "Ready?"

"For what?" Oliver asked.

"This is dumb," Sidney muttered.

Melissa leaned over her girl and whispered something.

Not Granger's problem. He was the host of this table — at least he felt like it — and conversation was up to him. "Okay, there are eight people around this table, and the word 'thankful' happens to have eight letters in it. Wendy, why don't you start, and we'll go clockwise? Name something you're thankful for that starts with the letter T. Faith, you're next with the letter H. Melissa, you've got A. Sidney is N, Oliver is K, I'm F, Pam has U, and Selah, you've got L. I'll give you a minute to think, then we'll go around the table."

Wendy shot him a deer-in-the-headlights look. He smiled at her and nodded. T had to be an easy one.

"Um..." She looked around, almost in panic. "T. I'm thankful for travel, since it means the girls could come visit me here."

Faith glanced at her mother. "H. I'm thankful for home."

Wendy visibly wilted as she gulped for breath and looked down.

"A?" Melissa asked. "Vowels are hard. Hmm. I'm thankful for an amazing dinner. Can I get away with that?"

Granger chuckled. "There are no rules. Sidney?"

"I have to be thankful for something that starts with N?"

He nodded.

"How about nothing?"

"That's not quite what I had in mind." He kept his voice gentle and conversational.

"How about nature?" Selah suggested.

"Sure." Sidney shrugged. "I hate nature, but whatever. I can pretend to like it."

That kid. Granger decided to let it go. "Oliver?"

"K?" The boy looked thoughtful. "I know! Kangaroos!"

Sidney rolled her eyes, but everyone else laughed. Maybe that would help break the ice, after all.

"My turn with F. I'm thankful for faith and for family." Granger turned to Pam.

"I'm with Melissa. Vowels are hard. I've got U, hmm? Maybe I'll be thankful for unicorns."

"But they're not real, Ms. Pam!" Oliver said.

"I didn't hear that in the rules."

"How can you be thankful for them if they're not real?"

Pam eyed the boy and tapped her chin. "Maybe because I'm thankful for imagination, but I got U instead of I? It's fun to imagine whimsical creatures, don't you think?"

"Yeah, maybe."

Poor kid still looked confused. Granger turned to Selah. "And L, for the grand finale?"

"I'm thankful for love." Her cheeks reddened.

Faith snickered.

Their mother turned to Selah. "What kind of love are we talking about?"

"I'm thankful for my boyfriend, Rex. But I didn't get B or R, so L for love it is."

"I didn't know you had a boyfriend."

"There are a lot of things you don't know, Mom."

Wendy's face shuttered as her shoulders slumped.

Granger's heart went out to her. The poor woman. From what Pam had said, Wendy's kids had mostly chosen to side with their father, even though he'd been the one to have an affair and initiate the divorce.

Laughter came from the tables around theirs, but here, humor did not exist.

He looked at the paper in his hand. Now what? There didn't seem to be any instructions in the event the icebreaker caused more chill than thaw.

Pam popped out of her chair. "Let me get started clearing the plates. We'll unveil the dessert table in a minute. It's already set up on ice."

Wendy surged to her feet. "I'll help."

Should Granger offer, too, or would he be of more use trying to keep the peace at the table?

Melissa turned to Selah. "Tell us about Rex! He must be a great guy. How did you meet?"

"He's in some of my college classes. He's pretty cool."

Wendy all but bolted with only a few plates in her hands.

Sidney leaned on the table. "Do you have a boyfriend, too, Faith?"

"Of course." The teen had an aura of superiority to her. What was she trying to prove to a tween? That she was so much better simply because she was four years older?

Granger wasn't impressed with Wendy's kids so far. But they were here with their mother, and that counted for something. Didn't it?

Melissa engaged the girls in conversation, so Granger rose and continued with clearing the table. Wendy and Pam had brought bins to the other tables, so the cleanup was fairly quick.

When Pam disappeared into the kitchen with a load, he took Wendy's bin and followed Pam. He set his load beside the dishwasher and sighed. "Wow, tonight could be going better."

Pam shook her head. "It sure could."

He reached for her, and she stepped into his arms. "It won't be long now before everyone leaves. I'll help you in here with the cleanup."

"Thanks. You don't have to do that."

"But I do." He kissed her lightly. "Because you're definitely the best part of my day."

"Today that might not be saying much."

Granger grinned and kissed her again. "That there is truth, but even if the kids weren't saboteurs, you'd *still* be the best part. Hands down. Always."

She leaned against his chest for a brief moment before pulling away. "Time to serve dessert."

She wasn't wrong, but they'd have time later.

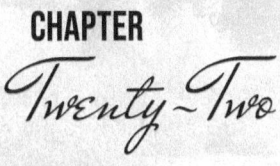

P am nestled against Granger on the love seat by the fireplace. She'd missed this over the past couple of weeks. It had all been her fault, second-guessing her right to be happy and find love.

Granger had been steadfast throughout. She didn't deserve him.

Satan is a liar.

May God always speak that reminder into her heart and mind. No one deserved goodness and happiness. That's why Jesus had come.

She tilted her face toward Granger. "Know what I'm thankful for?"

He pressed a kiss to her temple. "Hmm?"

"I'm thankful God speaks truth. I hope I keep listening."

"Our brains are finite."

She pondered his words. "And programmed to believe the superficial."

"What truths are you hearing from Him?"

"That's a hard question."

Granger rubbed his hand across her upper arm. How could

this man be so patient? He fully expected an answer, yet didn't seem in any hurry for her to deliver it.

"The lie I've believed is that it's all my fault."

"Anything specific?"

Pam let out a sharp laugh. "Yes and no? It's felt like my life pattern."

His soothing touch remained, as did his silence.

She'd come this far. She might as well get it all out. It would be easier if he rejected her now than later. It wasn't too late to finalize her notice to Julia and accept one of the other offers.

There was the old thought pattern again. How could she dig out its roots?

"My parents expected me to be perfect. To pursue excellence in everything, maybe because my sister did the opposite, and I had to be good enough for two daughters. Although believers, they were not in favor of me spending four years in Bible college. How could that set me up for the future? But I've never regretted it for a minute."

Hmm. She should have learned her lesson about pleasing her parents back then and saved herself thirty-some years of grief.

"They approved of Mark. He was a go-getter. I hid our problems from them as long as possible, because I knew they'd blame me. On the one hand, they pushed me to excel in my career but, on the other hand, they expected me to be the perfect little wife."

"The American dream, female version."

Pam blinked. "That's it, exactly. We're told we can do it all. Can be anything we want, but don't forget to excel at homemaking, too."

"It's a lot of pressure."

And she'd broken under it. "I was a terrible wife and mother."

Granger's grip on her shoulder tightened. "Remember who speaks the lies."

"I remember, but also, I was self-absorbed. It seemed easier to gain acclaim from my bosses and the public than from my parents, from Mark, from our kids."

He huffed a laugh. "I hear you. Relationships are hard. They're day in and day out."

"I don't blame Mark for leaving me. I wasn't easy to live with. The kids suffered, of course, but they were already suffering from my neglect and his... well, he neglected them, too. He was as focused on his career as I was on mine. We went from two ships passing in the night to shooting across each other's bows to trying to sink their battleships."

Granger's hand continued its soothing motion.

"I was selfish and mean," she whispered. "I deserved what happened."

"The accident wasn't a result of all that."

Pam tapped her head. "I know it up here, but my heart believes differently. If we hadn't split up, Mark wouldn't have been on the road that day, taking the kids to his parents' house."

"If you hadn't both been willing to try again, he wouldn't have been on the road that day."

She blinked. "Um... true."

"Accidents are just that. They're not justice. They're not punishment. They're not intended. They happen at random, to people who are happy and people who are sad. To people who are rich or poor. They are no respecters of persons."

Pam let out a long breath. "I know, but my programming says I deserve to be alone."

"God can override that thinking. Reprogram it."

"Do I have to be thankful for the accident?" Oh, no. Had she really said that out loud? "I know the Bible says to be thankful in all things, but how?"

There was silence for a long moment. Maybe she'd stumped him.

"I might be wrong, but I think the wording is *in* all circumstances, not *for* all circumstances. Was King David thankful that he committed adultery with Bathsheba and had her husband killed? Mark and your children died, but you didn't give the command.

David plotted Uriah's death in an attempt to cover up his first sin, adultery."

Pam had not taken aim at Mark's car that day. She'd been cautiously hopeful that their marriage might be salvageable. She'd wanted the children to have a good weekend with their grandparents while she and their father tried to work things out.

"I'm no great shakes to talk about this, Pam. I didn't even try to keep my marriage together. I let Denise make the call, and I believed her that it was better for me to quietly remove myself. It took years to realize she'd been absolutely wrong to cut me out of our daughter's life, and I'd been absolutely wrong to accept her choice without pushback."

Sometimes Pam forgot she wasn't the only one who'd screwed up. "I'm sorry," she whispered.

"Me, too." Granger tugged her closer and kissed her hair. "God reminded me that I can't go back and undo any of it. All I can do is accept my mistakes, ask forgiveness, and do the best I can now, with God's help."

"Where does thankfulness come into it?"

"I'm thankful for God's forgiveness. Psalm 103 says, 'as far as the east is from the west, so far does he remove our transgressions from us.' I was pondering that one day and realized if you keep going north, you will eventually pass the North Pole and start going south. But if you keep traveling east, you will never find yourself facing west. East and west never meet. Which means our sins cannot be located again. There are no lats and longs to pinpoint their location."

Pam had never thought of it that way.

"In Micah seven, we find that God has cast all our sins into the depths of the sea. Someone once told me God then put up a 'No Fishing' sign."

She managed a chuckle. "I like that visual."

"Me, too. But it's more than a visual. It's God's own truth."

A cell phone trilled. Must be Granger's, as Pam's was downstairs in her room.

He checked the screen and frowned. "It's Melissa. I need to take this."

"Hey, honey. What's up?"

A male voice cleared his throat. "This is Constable Jared from Jewel Lake Police Department."

Granger's veins filled with ice as he surged to his feet. Whatever was going on, he needed to face it standing up. "Why do you have my daughter's phone?"

"Your name and relationship to Melissa Everett?"

Hadn't he just said? "I'm Granger Durand. Melissa is my daughter. What's going on?"

"She was in an accident. She and two minor children have been transported to the hospital in Missoula."

He clutched the phone. Maybe if he held it tightly enough, he could keep a grip on the situation. "Status?"

"Melissa suffered minor injuries. Her son, Oliver, has a dislocated shoulder and several broken ribs."

"And Sidney?"

There was a slight hesitation. "She sustained the most injuries."

That covered nearly anything. "Which hospital?"

The constable named it.

"I'll be there in half an hour. Where will I find Melissa? And, once again, why are you calling from her number?"

"Her phone was found in the wreckage. It had been overlooked in the initial evacuation. You're listed as her emergency contact."

Granger's heart warmed at that.

"I'm sending her phone to the hospital first chance I get."

"Can I pick it up? Is it at the JLPD office?"

Muffled voices answered him. Perhaps the constable had covered the microphone for a moment.

"I understand you're retired armed forces?"

Whatever that had to do with anything. "Yes. Thirty years' service. Veteran of Iraq, Somalia, and Afghanistan. Why?"

"Stop by the accident site at the interstate onramp. I'll give it to you."

"Okay." Granger's head reeled. "Is there anything else I should know?"

"The car is totaled, just so you're prepared for the visual. We'll be here for a while yet piecing together what happened."

"On my way." Granger ended the call and pivoted to Pam. She'd risen and stood in front of the fireplace, clutching her arms around herself, her eyes wide. "Melissa and the kids were in an accident. I'm headed to the hospital." He hesitated. He couldn't ask Pam to accompany him. Too many memories would surge to the forefront.

She swallowed hard and raised her chin. "Want company?"

"I'd love it, but I don't want you traumatized."

Her laugh was sharp and humorless. "I'm already traumatized. I'm coming unless you forbid me."

"Never." His heart told him this would likely be a setback, but he couldn't refuse her.

"Do I have time to run downstairs and change into something more comfortable?"

She wore a dress and flats. He glanced down at himself. He wore dress pants, a button-down, and a loosened tie. "Five minutes. Meet you right here."

"You've got it." She jogged to the elevator. He took the stairs two at a time, wincing as his knee protested.

Pam, now wearing jeans and sneakers, stood in the lobby zipping up her jacket when he returned.

He blinked. "You were quick."

Her smile was fleeting. "I didn't want you to have a second thought about leaving me behind."

"I promised." But she was right. He'd have been antsy if he'd had to wait. He held out his hand and pushed the button to unlock the exit doors. "You should let Julia know why we're escaping."

Pam nodded. As soon as he'd settled her in his car, she pulled her phone out of her pocket, tapped in a message, then set the device in the console. She let out an audible breath. "May I pray?"

Granger's hands gripped the steering wheel as he sped toward the scene. "Please."

"Lord, You know far more than we do. I pray that You'll keep Melissa, Sidney, and Oliver in the palm of Your hand. Please, dear Jesus. Please."

"Amen." Granger cleared his throat. Already he could see flashing lights up ahead on the interstate approach. "Ready for this? The car is totaled. It's not going to be a pretty sight." He was reminding himself as much as her.

Pam fingers clenched in her lap. "I'm as ready as I'm going to get."

He pulled in behind the patrol car. "Wait here."

She nodded and closed her eyes.

Hopefully praying, not panicking, but she was an adult who'd chosen to come. He pushed out of the car and approached the scene. No amount of preparation could have readied him to see Melissa's car. Totaled was a complete misnomer for the amount of damage. It was a miracle anyone had survived at all. He took in the remainder of the scene where a semi-truck lay on its side, pointing the opposite way. Wasn't this the onramp? What had the truck even been doing on this section of road?

A police officer approached, silhouetted against the red-and-blue flashing lights. "Restricted area, sir. We're detouring traffic to the other interstate access on the east end of Jewel Lake."

"I'm Granger Durand. That's my daughter's car. Constable Jared said I could pick up Melissa's phone."

The man gave a sharp nod. "Be right back." True to his word, he was back in a flash and handed over the device. "Good luck."

"I don't need luck. God is in control."

"Right." The officer turned away.

Granger took one more scan of the scene, blew out a sharp breath, and returned to his car. He slid in and set Melissa's phone in the console. "I'm turning around. We need to use the other access."

"Is it… bad?" Pam's voice seemed distant and tiny.

He gulped as he backed the car in an arc. "Yes. It's bad, but they're alive. That's what counts."

"Okay." Pam leaned back against the headrest, eyes closed.

Hopefully praying. Granger was, too, but he needed to focus on the drive. One accident was more than enough for one night.

He could see becoming thankful for a collision like this, perhaps at some point in the future. At least, if Sidney came through the experience with no permanent damage. But Pam was reliving a similar situation with no survivors.

It must be vastly more difficult to give thanks for that.

It was like him being thankful for every casualty in war-torn countries. He'd personally inflicted death on enemy soldiers. He'd been honored to serve his country in the name of global peace, but thankful for each and every death? Not so much.

Granger navigated the eastern ramp onto I-90 and sped west toward Missoula. All he could do now was pray for his family… and for Pam, that this situation wouldn't bring her fragile healing to a screeching halt.

CHAPTER
Twenty-Three

P am shouldn't be here. This moment was for Granger and his family. She tried to hang back as they approached the emergency room, but Granger didn't relinquish his grip on her hand. Maybe her presence was for him rather than Melissa or the children. She could face her demons for him.

"Where can I find Melissa Everett?" Granger asked at the desk. "I'm her father."

"Let me check with her." The nurse headed into a nearby cubicle then returned with a nod. "She's okay with you coming in."

Pam pulled her hand away. "I'll wait out here."

Granger turned to her. "Please come with me."

"But, Melissa…" And Sidney. Sidney sneered at Pam. Hated her. But she was only a kid, and she'd suffered an untold amount this evening.

"I won't push you, Pam. I know this has to bring back horrible memories for you."

Pam gulped. "My family was brought directly to the morgue, not the ER."

Granger pulled her into his arms. "I'm so sorry. I shouldn't have asked you to come."

"You didn't. I offered." Why second-guess herself? Pam straightened her shoulders. "I'll come in, at least for a minute. If Melissa doesn't want me there, I'll understand and wait out here."

"Okay." He rested his hand on the small of her back as they entered the cubicle.

Melissa sprang to her feet and flung herself into Granger's arms. "How did you know?" she sobbed.

Pam hung back, scanning the single stretcher where Oliver lay, his eyes closed and his dark, curly hair like a halo on the thin pillow. Poor kid. But where was Sidney?

"You listed me as your emergency contact. When the police found your phone, they called me." Granger dug the device out of his pocket and handed it to his daughter.

"Good thing I did that." Melissa swiped tears from her eyes, which only smudged the dirt and blood on her face further.

"How's Sid?" Granger said quietly.

"They're doing an MRI. She was incoherent. Vomiting. Then..." Melissa's voice choked. "Then unresponsive."

"Brain bleed?"

Pam's heart constricted. She clutched her arms around herself when her entire body yearned to hold Melissa and relieve some of her agony. As though anyone could.

"That's what they're checking for. Oh, Dad. What will I do if she... if she dies?"

Granger's gaze latched onto Pam's across Melissa's shoulder. Somehow, he riveted her in place without a single touch.

"It was my fault. The accident. The two of them were bickering in the backseat, and I lost it. If I hadn't been distracted, I'd have seen that semi coming toward us in the wrong lane."

"It was *not* your fault." Granger spoke to Melissa, but he also spoke to Pam. "You weren't driving the semi."

At some point they needed to ascertain what had happened to the driver. Had he walked away without a scratch like the guy who'd taken Pam's family?

"Accidents are just that. They aren't premeditated. And they can't always be avoided. Is it okay if I pray for you and Oliver and Sidney right now?"

Pam knew he'd already been praying, and he wouldn't stop if his daughter declined his offer. This was simply for a verbal prayer.

"Sure. I could use a little divine assistance." Melissa's voice cracked.

Granger remained steady as he pleaded for God on his family's behalf, still holding his daughter in his arms.

Pam felt the solid foundation of his faith undergirding her. Did Melissa feel it, too? No doubt, his military training helped keep him calm in the face of trauma, but Granger clung to God in a way Pam had rarely witnessed before.

This was the man who'd chosen to love her, not that he'd told her in so many words. How could she not choose him back?

His steady, compassionate prayer continued, and Melissa's quaking shoulders steadied. On the stretcher, Oliver opened his eyes and surveyed them before focusing on Pam. His forehead tightened as he looked at her, like he couldn't quite place her.

Pam shifted closer. "Hey, good to see your eyes, buddy. How are you doing?" She kept her voice low so as not to disturb Granger and Melissa.

"Everything hurts."

"I bet it does."

"You're not my grandma, are you?"

It was Pam's turn to be confused. "No, I'm not. I'm not anyone's grandmother."

"Oh. Sidney said she wanted our old grandma. That she didn't want a new one."

Melissa leaned over Oliver. "She didn't mean it that way."

"Yeah, she did. She was yelling it. That's why you got mad."

The accident had been *Pam's* fault? And she hadn't even been there!

"That's not how it was." Melissa's eyes begged Pam not to take it personally.

Too late. Pam backed up. "I'll wait in the lobby."

Granger wrapped an arm around her waist. "Please," he whispered.

Just a moment ago, she'd wondered how she could ever walk away from him, but now she had to. Pam couldn't come into the middle of Sidney's irrational hatred.

"She hardly even knows my mother," Melissa pleaded. "Mom and Da…" She winced as she looked at Granger. "Mom and *Grant* have only visited two or three times in all the years we've been in Montana. Sidney doesn't even know what she's talking about."

"She said Grandma should come marry Gramps."

The nine-year-old couldn't seem to stop pouring gasoline on the fire.

"Grandma is married to Grandpa Grant. Even if Gramps wanted to marry Grandma Denise, he couldn't, because she's married to someone else."

Granger cleared his throat. "And I don't want to marry your grandmother. It's been a very long time since I've seen her, and…" He shook his head. "That's simply not something that will ever happen. Grownups need to be in love with each other to get married, and she's not whom I love." Granger held Pam close to his side. "This woman is. Pam Whorley."

Tears flooded Pam's eyes, and they weren't simply a result of excessive stimulation over the past few hours. The declaration of Granger's love had done it. To his grandson, no less.

"I'm happy for you, Dad." Melissa's gaze shifted back and forth between Pam and Granger. "Pam, you're great for him. Dad needs you. *We* need you. Even Sidney does. Please don't let her push you away."

"Thank you." Pam barely got the words out before she buried her face in Granger's shoulder. Poor man. His shirt was already soaked from his daughter's tears.

"I love you, Pam," he whispered.

Pam clung tighter. "Does she know… about my family?"

"I haven't told her. Do you want to?"

Not really, but perhaps she needed to. If things were to progress between them, Melissa would be part of Pam's future.

A nurse poked his head into the cubicle. "Mrs. Everett? We're taking Sidney up to the OR. Do you want to see her for a minute?"

Melissa gulped and followed the man out of the cubicle. Granger heard hushed voices outside, but his job remained in here. Holding Pam. Keeping an eye on Oliver.

Oliver frowned. "What's OR?"

Granger pulled Pam with him to the stretcher before grasping the boy's hand. "Operating room. The doctors will fix something that broke inside Sidney in the accident."

"She's broken?"

Granger managed a smile he didn't feel. "She has an injury inside her head they're going to fix." At least, that's what he thought would happen. Melissa would clarify when she returned.

"Oh." Oliver's eyelids shuttered.

Melissa ducked back inside.

If Granger didn't miss his guess, she barely held herself together. He held out his other arm, and she stepped into its shelter. "Results of MRI?"

"Confirmed brain bleed. They think they can fix it. What if they're wrong? What if she dies? I couldn't live with myself."

Good thing Oliver seemed to be asleep.

"Melissa?" Pam touched her arm. "Can I buy you a coffee? Maybe a snack?"

"No, I should…"

Granger squeezed his daughter. "Go with Pam. I'll stay here with Ollie so he won't be alone. Sidney is out of our hands right now and in God's. Go."

"Yeah. Maybe. I could use a few minutes. Call me if there's any word, Dad."

"Absolutely." He released both women and took a step back as their grasp on him fell away. "I'll just drag up that chair and sit by Ollie. Take your time. I imagine it will be a while, and I have a who-dun-it on my phone." Wow, it was going to be a late night. He definitely wouldn't be hitting the gym in the morning.

Pam reached for Melissa. "Come on. Let's go find the cafeteria. There must be one somewhere."

"You think it's open at this time of night?"

"We'll find out."

Granger dug his car keys out of his pocket and extended them to Pam. "In case you need to find someplace open nearby."

Her brows lifted then she nodded and took them. "Hopefully it won't be necessary. We'll ask at the desk and let you know if we're leaving the premises."

"Okay." He sat on the rigid plastic chair. The best that could be said for the thing was the ease of disinfecting it. And it was better than standing for an hour or two. Marginally.

The women left the space, and he took a long look at his grandson. The boy's chest rose and fell rhythmically. Natural sleep was good, right? Though they'd probably given him something for pain. A dislocated shoulder and a few broken ribs would take a few weeks to heal completely, but the kid would be fine.

His sister?

Granger leaned forward on his elbows and bowed his head. Sidney was in the surgeon's hands, but God guided those. Granger needed to hold the faith that God was in control.

Pam's words from earlier came back to him. Was one required to be thankful *for* moments like this? It was still Thanksgiving Day for another — he checked his watch — 28 minutes. While he hadn't been exactly trite in his gratitude earlier, the past hour or so had driven home, once again, how fragile life was.

God didn't cause accidents. He hadn't killed Pam's husband

and children. But it was still true that God took those circumstances and worked for the good of His people through them.

The who-dun-it could wait. Granger thumbed over to Romans eight in the Bible app on his phone. *And we know that for those who love God all things work together for good, for those who are called according to his purpose.*

His eyes drifted down the following verses. After mentioning troubles, famines, and wars, the writer said, *in all these things we are more than conquerors through him who loved us. For I am sure that neither death nor life, nor angels nor rulers, nor things present nor things to come, nor powers, nor height nor depth, nor anything else in all creation, will be able to separate us from the love of God in Christ Jesus our Lord.*

He read it through a few times. Each time, his heart swelled with trust and gratitude. The list missed nothing… and nothing could lessen God's love for him. For Pam. For Melissa or Ollie or Sidney.

More than conquerors.

He'd seen the change in Pam just today as she'd faced her fears of God's rejection.

There was that song they'd been practicing in worship team, "I am Loved" by Mack Brock. He opened it on YouTube and soaked in the affirming words. Like the song said, God's love changed everything, and Granger believed it. Received it. Was here for it.

He bowed his head. *Thank You, God.*

He prayed, once again, for the surgeons. Prayed for strength for Pam as she told her story. Prayed for his daughter to receive Pam's words and for Melissa's heart to soften to Jesus. Prayed for the boy on the stretcher beside him.

Prayed for himself, that God would renew his strength and give him wisdom.

Most of all, that he would never forget how much God loved him and wanted the best for him. Could times still be difficult?

Exhibit A: the accident tonight.

So, yes. But God would work everything out for good.

Even if Sidney died?

He couldn't bear to consider that outcome.

Help me trust You, Lord, even if it comes to that.

Granger needed God.

He kept on praying.

CHAPTER
Twenty~Four

H ave some more, little man."

Pam smiled as Julia encouraged Oliver at the lunch table. The two of them had fixed a few sandwiches for the staff, though Granger, Wendy, and Laura had already left to finish setting up the academy's gymnasium for tonight's outreach event.

His sandwich half eaten, Oliver pushed his plate away. "I'm not hungry."

"I never thought I'd hear a boy your age say that." Julia eyed him. "How about a cookie?"

"I could maybe make room for a cookie."

Julia rose and reached for the dessert plate. "Way to take one for the team."

"Huh?" Oliver eyed her with confusion.

"Never mind, Oliver." Pam brushed back his curls. It meant a lot that Granger had entrusted his grandson to her for a few hours. Melissa, of course, remained at Sidney's side in the hospital. "Mrs. Cox thinks she's being funny."

"I know I'm not funny." Julia shot her a look. "I'm trying to be encouraging. I'll see myself out." She headed back to the reception desk.

Oliver nibbled at the gingerbread man, but tears filled his eyes as he set it back down. "I want my mom."

Pam wanted to hug the kid, but with his arm in a sling to immobilize his shoulder, she didn't dare. "I know you do, honey. She's with Sidney, and she thought you'd like to stay here with your grandfather while she's busy."

"I know." He sighed. "But I miss her. I even miss my stupid, annoying sister."

"Sidney's getting better. She'll probably be home in a couple of days."

"Will she be nicer?"

"I can't promise that, honey. But maybe." At least, Granger had said his granddaughter's hostility had eased.

"I miss my dad, too." Oliver stared down at his plate. "How come he had to go away?"

"Aw, buddy." Pam crouched by his chair. Hadn't Roderick once asked nearly the same thing? "Grownups are complicated, but your dad still loves you."

"You think?" The boy's lip quivered.

"I'm certain of it." What was there not to love in this sweet child? Sure, Granger said that Chad had only returned a few times to see his kids since he'd left Melissa, but that didn't mean the man had forgotten he loved them.

After all, Mark had insisted he loved Courtney and Roderick, even while giving Pam the cold shoulder. Separation and divorce were so hard on kids. They either had to pick sides, like Wendy's kids, or their side was assigned to them by default, like Melissa's.

"When will Gramps be back?"

"In an hour or two." Pam eyed the boy. "How are you feeling? Do you want to lie down for a little while to rest up for this evening?"

"Do I have to go?"

Pam hesitated. "I think your grandfather will want you there. The food will be delicious." At least, if all the church women followed the recipes to a tee. They were likely doing that right this minute. Argh, Pam hated not doing her own cooking. She hated not being in control.

She blinked at the Christmas tree nearby.

Was that her problem? Control. She craved it. Always had. Everyone else would let her down. Even God. But she didn't do such a good job, either. She disappointed herself all the time. Who was she to think she could do a better job of controlling — managing — the universe than the infinite, all-powerful God who'd created it?

Ouch.

"It will be boring." Oliver flopped back in the chair dramatically then winced. "My shoulder hurts."

Pam glanced at the clock. "You can have another pill in 20 minutes. Your grandfather left me instructions."

"That's so long."

"Want me to read you a chapter of the Wilderking?" Pam had remembered how much Roderick had enjoyed the series, so she'd downloaded the first book, *The Bark of the Bog Owl*, and begun reading it to Oliver yesterday. Granger had picked up his own copy so they could tag team.

Ollie sighed. "Okay."

The reluctant acquiescence seemed to be code for a fist-pumping yes, but that probably didn't seem cool enough. "We'll go downstairs, okay? You can bring your gingerbread man if you like."

"I guess we can find out what Aidan and Dobro Turtlebane are up to." Oliver kept pace beside Pam as they walked to the elevator. He settled in on a comfy chair in the staff lounge as Pam thumbed open the ebook.

They were barely a few pages in when Faith entered the room and perched on the arm of another chair. "Is that Wilderking? I loved those stories when I was a kid! I must have read them ten times."

"Yes, we're reading the first one."

"That kid — Aidan? Was so brave." Faith chuckled. "I always wanted to be brave like him."

Oliver studied Faith. "He has adventures with Dobro."

"And my life was *so* boring." The girl sighed. "You, too?"

Oliver shrugged. "I sure don't live in a swamp and have a feechie for a friend. And I'm not a Wilderking."

"Yeah, Aidan's adventures were way more fun than my life, too. Imagine a truth sayer telling you you're going to be a king!"

"Girls can't be kings."

Faith tossed her hair. "In stories, we can be anything at all."

"In real life, too," Pam interjected. "Whatever God calls us to do, He'll help us accomplish it if we ask Him."

"Right, the Wilderking stories are really about King David from the Bible." Faith turned back to Oliver. "Do you go to Sunday school? Do you know about David?"

"I've heard of him. He killed a giant! But I want to hear this story."

Faith mimed zipping her mouth shut. "May I listen, too, Aunt Pam?"

"Sure. I'll get Ollie his pain meds first, then we'll carry on." Pam rose to get the boy a glass of water and a pill.

Her phone rang, and she glanced over. Melissa! She hadn't heard directly from Oliver's mom before, even though they'd exchanged phone numbers in the hospital cafeteria Thursday night. "It's your mom, Oliver. Take your meds while I talk to her." She tapped to activate the call. "Hi, Melissa!"

"Hey, Pam. Dad says you've got Ollie for the afternoon. I can't thank you enough."

"It's no trouble. I'm not cooking at the inn tonight, since we're closed for the outreach dinner."

"I know I told Dad I couldn't make it, that I need to stay with Sidney, but do you think I can change my mind?"

"Sure. Give him a call. He's at Creekside setting up."

"He didn't pick up. I'll try him again in a bit."

Pam's grip tightened around the phone. "Sidney's okay with you stepping away for a couple of hours?"

"Yeah. She's sleeping a lot, but the doctors think they fixed the bleed, and she'll be okay. She just needs a lot of rest."

Pam glanced over to where Faith and Oliver seemed deep in discussion on the Wilderking story. "I'm so glad to hear that. I've been praying for her. For you."

"Thanks. I wasn't so sure about God, but maybe He's coming through for me. For my kids."

Pam let out a long breath. "You know what I've learned?"

Silence for a moment. "I'm so sorry, Pam. That was an insensitive thing for me to say."

"No, it's okay." Strangely, it was. "I've learned that even when God doesn't answer my prayers the way I wanted, He's *still* come through for me. He still loves me. He still has my best at heart."

"That's so hard."

"It is. I'm not trying to put a happy face on a bleak situation. But God's love… it simply remains. It's not dependent on circumstances." Oh, how she wished she'd seen that years ago. Better late than never?

"Thanks, Pam. I'm so glad you're in my dad's life. See you tonight."

Granger took a long look around Creekside Academy's gymnasium before flipping off the bank of light switches, one by one. Eli's team of youth had done an admirable job of helping out. The women of the church, with help from some of the men, had come through with delectable food. The gorgeous, festive trees had been gifted to a dozen thrilled families — the Cavanagh men would deliver them tomorrow. Laura had led a carol sing and sang a couple of solos — Granger overheard Caleb afterward, asking if she'd sing with the worship team.

Wendy came toward him, zipping up her parka. Everyone else had already left. "That went well."

"It did. I couldn't be more happy with the results."

"I'm glad your daughter could come, after all. Your grand-daughter is stable?"

"Huge answer to prayer on both those counts." Melissa had seemed captivated by Eli's brief Christmas message. Granger hadn't had a chance to speak with her afterward. She'd been in a hurry to return to Sidney's side, and Granger had still been on the clock. "Ready to go?"

"Yes, I think so. The volunteers were great. The kitchen is clean."

"They did well. The whole congregation really pulled togeth-er." He held the door for Wendy then locked up the building before following her to his car.

She slid into the passenger seat before he arrived, so he started the vehicle and backed out of his parking spot. It had snowed while they were inside, but the roads didn't seem too slick.

He glanced over. "When do your girls fly back to Portland?"

"Tomorrow afternoon. I wish I'd had more time to spend with them."

"If I'd have known they were coming, I'd never have asked you to help me plan this shindig."

"Don't be silly. Planning things is what I do best." He barely heard her muttered finale: "It's results I can't manage."

"Hey. Am I hearing self-trash-talk?"

"No?"

"Sounded like it from here."

Wendy let out a tiny sigh. "It's not trash talk if it's true."

"Whose truth do you believe?"

Silence, so he pressed on.

"I know you're a Christian, which makes you an overcomer. Not someone who hopes to conquer or even plans to conquer, but someone who does it." He glanced over at her. Man, he was in over his head. He didn't know Wendy all that well, but maybe God had put them together for this event so he could speak some truth into her life.

"I've been camped out in Romans 8 a lot lately," he went on.

"And we know that for those who love God, all things work together for good."

"That verse, and the ones following. I'm thinking specifically of verse 37. 'In all these things, we are more than conquerors through him who loved us.'"

"Overcoming is for other people, not failures like me."

"Wendy, you do know that's not true, right? God loves you."

"Dave doesn't."

"Dave's one man, and a selfish one, at that." Granger would like to give the dude a piece of his mind on tossing his wife aside. Yeah, no doubt the story was much more involved, but still. The guy had an affair and, from what Granger had seen, turned their kids against their mother. That took a special kind of nastiness.

"It's just hard, you know? Why am I not lovable? I'm not asking like I want you to love me instead of Pam. Not that at all, but she's lucky to have you."

"I'm blessed to have found her. But I'm sure there is a man out there who will love you not only in spite of your perceived failures, but maybe because of them."

The sound she emitted was somewhere between a snort, a snicker, and a sob. "I doubt it. I had my chance, but I wasn't good enough."

It wasn't Granger's job to convince her otherwise. He couldn't be that person in her life. Didn't want to be. But he couldn't sit back and not even try to counter the lies. "You are worthy, Wendy. Dig into scripture until you believe it."

She shrugged one shoulder and looked out the window on the other side as they turned past the Happy Trails Stables sign.

"I know Julia asked you ladies to commit to three months. Are you considering staying longer?"

"I might as well. There's nothing for me in Oregon. Even my kids don't want me."

Patience. "Pam and I will keep praying for you."

"Thanks."

He pulled into the circular drive and stopped at the inn's main doors. "Be careful out there. It might be slippery."

"Thanks for the ride, Granger. I appreciate it." She climbed out of the car, shut the door, and walked toward the doors, her shoulders slumped.

"Lord? Please remind Wendy of Your love. Give her hope for her future."

He drove around to the parking lot and locked the car before entering the inn. Pam did not await him by the fireplace. Wendy, too, was long gone.

But, tomorrow was a new day.

CHAPTER
Twenty-Five

P am studied the townhouse from the comfort of Granger's car. "This is it, huh?"

"This is it. I... I hope you like it."

So did she. "I definitely want the grand tour." She reached for the handle, but Granger touched her knee.

"I'll get that."

Mark had never opened doors for her. Truth? Pam probably wouldn't have let him. She was a self-made woman and all that. Blah, blah, blah. How things had changed.

Granger opened the car door, grasped her hand, and helped her out before wrapping his arm around her back. "It hadn't snowed last time I was here."

"When do you take possession?"

"Technically, tomorrow, but they snuck me the keys early. There will be some scrubbing and painting before I move in. Julia's happy to let me stay at Maranatha a little longer."

Pam chuckled. "I bet she is. Not that she's mercenary."

He laughed. "No. She's more like a mother bird who takes in strays and wants everyone contented and safe in her nest."

"That about sums her up." Pam took in the white clapboard siding and dark blue window trim. "It looks well kept up."

"The owners did a lot of work to it about eight years ago when their mother moved in."

"She's in a nursing home now?"

"That's what they said. So…" He unlocked the front door and ushered Pam inside. "Remember the furniture was picked by or for an octogenarian. I'm not sure what to keep, what to toss, or what to use until I can replace it. I'd love advice on that."

Pam toed off her snowy boots and turned slowly. "Are we talking about that floral armchair?"

"Maybe?"

She laughed as she crossed the space and settled into the chair. "It's comfy."

"Then maybe it can stay, at least for a while. But I really want to know what you think of the kitchen."

She looked in that direction to see white, farmhouse-style cabinetry with a cobalt blue countertop. It could be worse. She strolled over and took in the compact layout. The window over the sink looked into the front yard. The appliances could use an upgrade, for sure, but maybe they'd be fine for Granger. How much did the man cook? He seemed competent the times he'd helped her at the inn.

"Tell me the truth." He leaned against the wall.

"Well, it depends." She chuckled. "The layout isn't terrible, but is installing a gas range an option? Gas is so much more responsive than electric."

"I thought induction was all the rage."

She wrinkled her nose. "It is, but I prefer gas."

"The fireplace runs on it, so I imagine it's doable." He studied the kitchen then looked at her. "Anything else? Paint? New countertops?"

Pam hesitated. "It depends on your personal esthetic."

"What if I wanted it to depend on *your* preferences?"

If that were true, wouldn't he have shown her the unit before he bought it? Maybe the thought was unfair. Two weeks ago when he'd placed his offer, she'd still been ready to bolt for

Charleston at the slightest provocation. She'd been unable to believe a man like Granger could want a permanent relationship with her. She'd been unable to trust God desired that, either.

"Honey?" Granger pulled her into his arms and pressed a kiss to her forehead. "Your thoughts, please."

"I guess it depends… on us."

He tipped her chin up so she had little choice but to meet his gaze. "I want there to always be an us. I want to cook with you in this little kitchen."

Was that a proposal? Not quite. They'd only met two months ago, after all. Still, maybe no one would fault people in their 50s for being sure more quickly. "I'm bossy in the kitchen."

"You're bossy outside the kitchen, too." The laugh lines around his eyes crinkled. "I kind of like a woman who takes charge."

"Do you now?"

"Yes—"

But she cut off his response by accepting the challenge. She grabbed his shirt collar, rose on tiptoes, and pressed her lips to his.

Granger gathered her flush against him and deepened the kiss.

She lost herself in the sensations provoked by his mouth, sensations she'd long buried and forgotten. Could she truly be desirable again? Could she merge her life with Granger's the way their bodies melded right now?

Could she trust Granger with her heart?

Too late. He already owned it and treated it with the utmost care and compassion. Her heart swelled with gratitude, love, and, yes, yearning. God had given her another chance. She wouldn't treat it lightly.

Breathless, Pam pulled away slightly. "I love you, Granger Durand."

His dark eyes met hers, full of honesty and passion. "I love you, Pamela Whorley."

"Show me the rest of your home." Otherwise they'd spend so

long kissing in the kitchen that his daughter would be waiting for them to pick Oliver up again. Melissa needed to get back to Sidney's side, but she'd craved some downtime at home with her boy.

Granger grinned and kissed Pam's nose. "Your wish is my command. You see the kitchen, dining area, and living room. Down the hallway, there are two bedrooms, two bathrooms, a laundry room, and a door to the patio. Now, can I kiss you again?"

Pam set both hands on his chest and pushed him away. "In a minute." He kept reaching for her hips, but she took a step back, laughing. "Let me go look!"

"Okay, fine. I'll keep my hands to myself." He stuffed them deep in his jeans pockets, stared at the ceiling, and whistled nonchalantly.

This man.

How could he love her? And yet she knew he did. Knew she loved him in return with all the intensity and resolve her 50-plus years had given her. She poked into the smaller of the two bedrooms, perfect for when one of the grandchildren stayed over. The master bedroom was larger than she'd expected, and completely void of furniture. "This room is empty?"

Granger's laugh rumbled. "I refuse to sleep in some little old lady's twin-sized hospital bed."

That caught her funny bone, and she chuckled, too.

"To say nothing of her dark walnut antiques that reminded me of my own grandmother's house from way back. I sent this room's furnishings with the woman's son. Maybe they were family heirlooms. If not, that's his problem."

"It's a big room."

Granger slipped his arm around her waist from behind. "Big enough for a king and a few dressers and such. Look, two walk-in closets and an ensuite. They removed the tub and put in a zero-threshold shower, but I prefer a shower to a soak, anyway. Maybe that's from my years in the military. Besides, the other bathroom has a tub in case anyone cares."

"I'm a shower person myself."

"I knew I loved you for a reason."

She arched her brows. "That's the reason?"

"Uh, not the only one."

Pam laughed and poked her head into the master bath. The shower was massive, plenty big enough for two people. Um... her mind should not be going there. Not at this stage, for sure. "Nice bath." She backed out, her face burning.

If Granger noticed, he said nothing, just returned her to the hallway, where they peeked out the back door to the patio and fire pit, both coated with a few inches of snow. "I think that will be a great spot for a morning coffee in the summertime."

Hmm. She could see that, too. "It looks idyllic."

"My whole life looks that way."

Pam liked the house.

Granger blew a sigh of relief. He'd waffled between thinking she'd never take a chance on him to holding his faith that they were meant to be.

Faith was winning. Had already won. He just needed to figure out what he was going to do about it and when. Besides soon. That was a given.

He'd kissed Pam goodbye on the inn's front steps then driven to the hospital. Melissa's insurance had kicked in with a car rental, and she'd decided to take Oliver to see his sister. Granger would bring the boy back to Jewel Lake later. Melissa expected Sidney's doctor to discharge her in the morning, so long as the girl took it easy for a few weeks.

Sidney grumbled that she hated missing her figure skating recital, but that couldn't be helped. At least she was alive and hadn't seemed to incur any permanent injury. She'd be missing school until the new year, though. Brains needed low-stress time to heal.

Granger jingled his keys in his pocket as he made his way into the hospital.

And that, right there, was his problem. He wanted to propose to Pam, but last he'd heard, Sidney had been vehemently opposed. While he didn't intend to let a 12-year-old determine her grandfather's life choices, this might not be the moment to stress her out.

What to do? "God?"

Granger's prayer life was definitely getting a workout the past couple of months. More specifically, the last few days.

And we know that for those who love God, all things work together for good.

He did know that. He clung to it. He'd nearly memorized the remainder of the chapter, as well, since he'd read the verses so many times.

Granger let himself into Sidney's room, where she was reclining in bed, leaning against an array of pillows. "Hey, Sid." He bent over and kissed her cheek. "How's my girl?"

"I'm okay, Gramps." Her dark eyes met his with less attitude than he'd seen since arriving in Jewel Lake a few months back.

"Really okay?" He gripped her hand, and her fingers curled around his.

"Yeah. Mom says…" Sidney looked past him to where Melissa surged out of a visitor's chair.

"Ollie and I are taking a walk. Want something from the vending machine?"

"Chips?" Sidney sounded hopeful.

"You've got it. We'll be right back." Melissa gave a significant look at Granger before hauling her son out the door.

Granger settled on the edge of the bed. "What was all that about?"

"Mom said I need to talk to you."

"Oh, yeah? What about?"

Sidney sighed. "Your girlfriend."

Granger blinked. "Pam." Just to clarify.

"Yeah." Sidney picked at the nubbly texture of the hospital blanket. "Mom said my grandma isn't coming back."

"She might come to visit." Not that Granger kept in touch with Denise, but wouldn't she want to see her daughter and grandkids occasionally? Melissa had mentioned two half-siblings, so maybe Denise's children with Grant took precedence.

"Maybe. But she won't marry you."

"That is true." And Granger wasn't the slightest bit sad about that.

"Mom said Ms. Pam is really nice and that her own kids died in a car crash a long time ago."

"Also true." Granger gulped.

"And Mom said Ms. Pam makes you happy, and I should try to like her."

"I'd really appreciate it if you did. I promise, if you give her a chance, you'll like her a lot. I do."

"Ollie, too. She's even reading him a chapter book!"

Granger grinned. "Pam and I are taking turns. It's an exciting story, and both of us want to read it, too."

"Maybe someone could read to me?" Sidney sounded wistful.

"I'd love to. I can read you that one, or something else. Whatever you want."

"Ollie says Ms. Pam is a better reader than you are." Sidney peeked up at him through her lashes.

He slapped his hand across his chest, feigning dismay. "I'm so hurt!"

"Are you, Gramps?"

"Not at all." He chuckled. "Pam's a great reader. She does all the voices. I'm not so good at those." He squeezed Sidney's hand. "She'd be honored to read to you."

"You think?"

"I know it." Granger studied his granddaughter's face. "What would you think if I asked Ms. Pam to marry me?"

"Would that make her my grandma?"

"Only if you want her to be. That would be up to you and her."

Melissa squealed from over by the door. "Did I hear what I think I heard? You're going to propose to Pam! When? How? Can I help? Me and the kids?"

Granger blinked as his daughter threw herself at him. He barely managed to keep from collapsing on top of Sidney. "Um, I don't have a plan. Not yet."

"We'll help you make one, right, kids?" She held up a palm and Oliver slapped it. She turned to Sidney, who offered a half-hearted tap. "We've got this, Dad."

CHAPTER
Twenty-Six

Melissa waved at Pam from a small table in the Copper Carafe. "I'm glad you could make it!"

"Thanks for the invitation." And Pam could be thankful Melissa hadn't insisted on her first choice of the Golden Grill. She still couldn't bring herself to relax in that venue. Melissa had already ordered the sandwich and a coffee Pam had picked from the online menu, so Pam slipped into the chair across from Granger's daughter.

"I wanted to talk to you without little ears. Or big ones."

Intriguing. Pam joined Melissa's chuckle. "Your dad is enjoying all the time he's spending with the kids while you're at work."

"I'm so thankful for him. I don't know what I'd do without him here. It's weird. I didn't want him. Didn't think I needed him." Melissa shook her head. "But here we are, and I was wrong."

"It's hard being a single mom." And Pam had only done the gig for a few months.

"I didn't mean to throw your memories under the bus."

"Melissa?" Pam waited for the younger woman to meet her gaze before continuing. "Please don't ever regret talking about your kids... or mine. I blocked off that part of me for too many years, not realizing how healing openness could be. While I can't exactly say I'm thankful they died—"

"Of course not!"

"Here's the thing, though. Gratitude changes everything."

Melissa tilted her head to one side. "What do you mean?"

"God uses our life experiences to make us who we are. If we cede over control — I admit that's a hard one — He takes all the mess, everything, and works it out for our good."

"Dad said something about that the other day. He was quoting the Bible, I think."

"He keeps reminding me, as well. It's in Romans 8:28: 'And we know that for those who love God, all things work together for good.'"

"Well, that lets me out, then. I don't love God."

"You could. It's worth it."

"I don't know. That little sermon at the dinner made me think, though."

"The Bible also says that if we seek for God, we'll find Him. He's the Creator of the universe, but He wants to have a relationship with us."

"Yeah, sounds good, but I'm not so sure. Evolution is a thing, you know."

"So I've heard." Pam chuckled. "But I think it takes more faith to believe in evolution than in creation."

"How's that?" Melissa had a sip of coffee.

Pam pulled her cell phone from her purse and laid it on the table. "Tell me. How likely is it that somehow, randomly, all the tiny pieces in this device bumped into each other out there." She waved heavenward. "They just so happened to collide and form this phone. Not only that, but it isn't a dummy phone, and it isn't the only one. There are millions just like it, and they can communicate with each other. They can call up any kind of information you can dream of. But it was just a happy accident."

Melissa shook her head. "That's ridiculous."

"I know, right?" Pam lifted her sandwich and had a bite. Chewed it slowly, swallowed, and took another, while Melissa frowned at her. Hopefully thinking the little analogy through.

"Humans are more complex than cell phones," Melissa said at last.

Pam nodded.

"So, you're saying that it's easier to believe in God."

"It's easier for me. Still a stretch, I'll grant you that. But one or the other must be true, right? Because the universe had to come from somewhere. Accidents are random." She paused. Wow, that was so true. The one that had taken Mark and the children had come out of nowhere and changed the course of her history. The one that had stopped Melissa's family in its tracks had also been random. The truck driver had fallen asleep at the wheel, certainly not by choice.

Pam shook her head to dislodge the thoughts. "But God is orderly. He has a plan and a purpose for creation, for all of us, and that is far more comfort to me than thinking I live in a colossal happenstance."

"It's still a stretch to believe. Maybe you're delusional."

"I know I'm not."

"How can you be sure?"

Pam pressed her palm over her heart. "Years ago, I asked God to show me if He was real, and He did. I can't explain it so you will understand, though there are books out there that clearly lay out the evidence. But in my heart of hearts, God stilled all my objections and my unbelief, and I know He is real."

"Wow." Melissa picked a few crumbs off of her mostly uneaten sandwich. "I'll have to think about that but, believe it or not, I didn't ask you to meet me for a debate on existential life questions."

"No?" Pam laughed. "What then?"

"It's my dad's 60th birthday the Sunday before Christmas, and I thought it would be fun to throw a party for him. He said he's hoping to have his place ready to move into by then, so maybe a combination birthday and housewarming party?"

"A party? Count me in!"

"I figured you'd want to brainstorm with me. Do you have any ideas that sprang to mind?"

"You first. It was your idea."

"You've heard my entire thought process. Dual party." Melissa held up both hands. "I'm no planner. Over to you."

"Organizing stuff is what Wendy does best."

"Newsflash." Melissa leaned closer and lowered her voice. "My dad's not into Wendy."

"Okay, so my ideas? Food, of course. We can do a tapas bar. I could prep everything at the inn and lay it out in his kitchen."

"Of course, food. That sounds great. Does Sunday afternoon sound okay?"

Pam poked in her phone's calendar app. "Sure. It looks clear. Who all do you want to invite?"

"You know better than I do who he'd want there."

"It's not that big a space." Pam bit her lip. "Some of the gang from Maranatha Inn, of course. A few people from the church. Maybe two dozen, total?"

"I guess we'll need chairs. And to think Dad got rid of that floral monstrosity."

Pam laughed. "The church has a bunch of folding chairs. I'm sure Eli could arrange for some to be brought over."

"Decorations?"

"That is totally in your court. Except your dad and I did talk about setting up a Christmas tree that weekend, so you can go from there."

"One more thing."

Pam could think of a dozen items that still needed to be decided upon. "Hmm?"

"Can you keep this a secret?"

"Yes! I love surprises. Good ones, at least."

"Me, too." Melissa grinned like the Cheshire Cat and rubbed her hands together. "I might have to take this sandwich to go."

"We're on." Melissa's voice rang triumphantly as she came through the door after work.

"Did she suspect anything?" Granger wanted to know.

"I don't think so. I asked if she could keep a secret, and she seemed eager to do that. I definitely didn't tell her we had an ulterior motive for the party."

He chuckled and set his book aside. Both kids were watching a movie in the other room. "So, what's she taking on? Food, I imagine. I think that's her love language."

"Yes to the food. She said you two plan to set up a Christmas tree that weekend. Saturday, I'm hoping, since we're shooting for a Sunday afternoon party."

Granger's imagination saw him and Pam cozied up by the fireplace with a hot chocolate, the lights from his tree providing ambience. He couldn't wait.

"Dad?"

He blinked. "Yes, we can have the tree up Saturday. The flooring guys had an unexpected opening and can install the laminate next week. Then I can start bringing in furnishings. I've already begun transferring my lease in Carlisle to my friend, and he's going to ship my boxes of dishes and stuff like that. I don't have a lot, so I'll still need to go shopping."

"Pam might want to help."

"But right before Christmas? Everything is so busy at the inn. The place is bustling."

"Trust me. She wants to spend time with you. Plus, it's going to be her home, too."

"If she says yes."

Her eyebrows popped up. "Do you have any reason to think she'll turn you down? Because if you do, you shouldn't be planning a proposal in front of all her friends."

"This shindig is all your idea, not mine."

"Is the concern real? I need to know."

Granger shook his head. "Nothing's a sure thing until it's a sure thing but, no, I'm not worried. We're on the same page."

"Whew. You had me panicking for a minute there."

"I'm sorry. Your old dad has butterflies in his stomach just thinking about taking such a life-altering step. Pam is amazing. You're going to love her."

"I already do. She's so gracious, and after all she's been through…"

"She's come out the other side victorious. It's been hard."

"She told me a lot of her story last week in the hospital. I can't tell you how grateful I am that our story — mine and the kids — had a different ending than her family's."

"I'm thankful, too. I've only just found you and those two scoundrels. I want to be part of your lives for a very, very long time."

Melissa stepped into his arms, and he hugged her tightly.

"Me, too, Dad. I want that, too. Mom has no idea what she gave up when she ditched you."

Granger relinquished his hold. "It was a difficult time, for sure. We've been over that, you and me. But now, looking back? I'm thankful. God has worked all things—"

"Pam said the same verse."

He chuckled. "It's kind of become our thing, Pam's and mine."

"Because you both believe in God."

"Yes." Granger studied his daughter.

"She talked to me. I'll think about it. That's all I can promise right now."

Pam had witnessed to his daughter about her faith? His heart swelled. If he'd ever doubted Pam was the woman for him — and he hadn't — any qualms were now resolved. She was amazing, and she fit, not just with him, but with his family. "Let me know if you have questions."

"Pam said that, too."

He nodded. "Or you can talk to her. Maybe come to church with us sometime?"

"Not on your birthday. I'll be in the townhouse getting ready for your party."

Should they choose a different time instead?

Melissa held up a hand. "I know what you're thinking, and no. Pam's schedule is packed, but she has Sunday afternoon open, literally from one to four. We're not moving a thing. Not unless you're getting cold feet."

"My feet have never been toastier. I'm running on hot sand here."

"TMI, Dad. I'm not sure I needed to know that."

Too much information? Nah. The line was nowhere near there. "Chad didn't deserve you," Granger said softly. Not that he'd ever met the guy who'd been his son-in-law.

She shrugged. "But I love my kids, so there's that."

"I get it. That's kind of how I feel about your mother."

"Life is complicated."

"You can say that again."

Melissa looked around. "Where are the kids?"

"I introduced them to *The Princess Bride*. I can only read aloud for so long before I lose my voice."

"I can see Ollie like the bedridden boy, going 'ugh' at the kissing but enthralled with the sword fights."

"Nailed it."

"Okay, dinner. Want to stay?"

"No, I'm headed out. Check your oven. The casserole in there should be ready in ten."

She sniffed the air. "That's what I smell! You didn't have to do that."

"Don't get used to it. I'm not promising to cook every day I'm here with the kids."

"Just two weeks until winter break, then I get some time off. They should both be ready to go back when school resumes."

Granger reached for his coat. "I'll be here in the morning. See you then."

"You're a lifesaver."

"You're confusing me with Jesus."

"As if." She rolled her eyes. "I'm aware you're not perfect."

"I don't need to know what your first clue was. Love you, honey. Good night."

"Need a Pam fix?" Melissa called after him.

"You bet your boots, I do." And he closed the door behind him.

CHAPTER
Twenty-Seven

Granger glanced up as the lights went out in the kitchen across the inn's public spaces. *Go time.* Melissa would be disappointed, but that wasn't his problem.

This time, this place, had become his and Pam's special moment for closing out their day. He always fixed two mugs of hot chocolate from the dispenser beside the front desk at ten pm. He always waited by the fireplace, a Christmas carol playlist providing a quiet backdrop.

He rose as Pam swished through the swinging doors, lit by the three Christmas trees in the lobby. "Hey, sweetheart."

"Hey, yourself." She stepped into his arms and stayed there for a long moment.

He could feel the tension easing from her body as he held her close. "Long evening?"

"You could say that. But it's over, and we've got reduced hours until the new year. I can't say I'm sad about that."

"Julia's just happy you're staying on. She can afford to give you a breather over the holidays."

"I'm happy I'm staying on, too." Pam looked up at him.

All the invitation he needed. He lowered his head and kissed her, pouring all his emotions into the connection. When God invented kissing, He'd known what He was doing. Finally, Granger pulled away enough to rest his forehead against hers. "I love you, Pam."

"Love you more."

"Not possible."

"Hmm. Maybe it doesn't need to be a competition."

He chuckled. "Not everything needs to be. Who knew?"

"Right?" She stretched to give him a peck on the lips.

"I can't imagine my life without you, Pam. I'm thankful every minute of every day that God brought both of us here to Jewel Lake."

"A man from Pennsylvania and a woman from South Carolina, meeting in Montana. That was extravagant of Him."

"Wasn't it, though? Guess that proves He works everything together for good."

"I'm thankful."

"Me, too." He took a deep breath and let it out slowly. "I'll be moving into my house on Monday."

"I'll miss our rendezvous when I close the kitchen."

"I can keep coming. This is my favorite time of day." That used to be his early morning workout routines, but they'd shifted later in the day and were no longer the highlight. He'd kept the habit, though.

"That's asking a lot."

"You didn't ask. I offered. But I thought of a solution."

"A solution?" She looked up at him, the glimmering candle-light from the fireplace mantel reflecting in her eyes.

Granger nodded as he grasped the back of the love seat and lowered himself to one knee. He'd practiced, trying to keep the knee loose. "Will you marry me, Pam? I love you so much. Join me in that little townhouse. Keep working for Julia as long as you want to, but come home to me. Please, Pam? Marry me?"

He picked up the little box he'd left on the love seat and opened it toward her.

Pam's eyes widened as she clapped her hand over her mouth. "Granger, I... I can't believe this."

His knee hurt. "Please say yes?"

"Yes!" She stretched both hands toward him, helping him back to his feet.

Whew, his fear his knee would cave in had been unfounded. He tugged the ring from its cozy nest, reached for Pam's left hand, and slipped it into place on her third finger. It was a tiny bit loose, but the jeweler could take care of that.

"It's beautiful, Granger. Thank you."

The lighting was too dim for her to see it clearly, but that didn't make her wrong. It was a slim, stunning, platinum band with inset diamonds. He'd specifically asked the jeweler what he'd recommend for a chef.

Granger gathered her into his arms again and kissed her. Somehow it felt different with this promise between them.

Finally, he pulled away with a chuckle. "Melissa's going to kill me."

"Why? She's not in favor?" Pam sounded apprehensive.

"She loves you. She's definitely in favor, as are the kids. Both of them."

"Okay?"

"It's just..." Well, he'd gone this far, he might as well tell the rest of the tale. "She's gone to a lot of work to plan a party for tomorrow afternoon."

"You know about that?"

Granger laughed. "Sure do. She was basically planning a proposal party."

"Not a birthday or housewarming party like she told me? And asked me to keep it a secret from you, I might add."

"She's a sneaky one, my daughter. But I didn't want a couple of dozen witnesses. That house is nothing special yet, not like our spot here by the fireplace. This seemed like the best setting, the best time. But she's still going to kill me for spoiling her fun."

"She'd make a good double agent." Pam nestled against Granger's chest.

"Yes, she's devious that way."

"But you out-sneaked her."

"Well, I can't have my kid telling me what to do and how to do it. That's no way to start a new chapter in my life. A new chapter where she, Sidney, and Oliver are secondary characters, but you and me? We're the stars. We're the ones the chapter is all about."

"And God," Pam reminded him. "Because without Him, we'd still be in Pennsylvania and South Carolina."

"He's not a character, though. He's the author, and I love the story He's writing."

"Some of the earlier chapters were hard."

Granger pressed a kiss to her forehead. "Yes. There will almost certainly be some hard chapters ahead, too. They say growing old isn't for sissies."

"True. But hopefully, there will be plenty of good years before that happens."

"No guarantees. None except Romans 8:28." And he kissed her.

The door to Granger's townhome opened as they drove up, and Melissa leaned against the jamb with her arms crossed.

Uh oh. "She doesn't look too happy." Pam reached for the door handle.

"Hey, how many times do I have to tell you to wait for me to come around the car?" Granger chuckled. "I texted Melissa last night and told her I'd chosen my own program."

Pam folded her gloved hands in her lap. "And she said?"

"A lot of things, but she's over it."

"She doesn't look over it." But she spoke to an empty car, since Granger was on his way around.

He opened her door with a bow, held his hand for her, and pulled her close for a second. "One day I'll carry you over the threshold, but not today."

She tipped up an eyebrow. "Are you sure your knee is up for it?"

"I'll keep working out."

Pam groped his bicep through his jacket. "You do that. I can't complain at the results."

Granger smirked.

"Coming in, or are we heating the entire town?"

"Such impatience," Granger murmured, but he took Pam's hand as they strolled up the sidewalk.

Someone had shoveled away the snow — Melissa? — and with today's sunshine, it seemed unlikely they'd get covered again in the next few hours.

Pam released Granger's hand and reached for his daughter. "I hope you're not too upset with your father."

The woman shook her head with a rueful chuckle. "We'd made such big plans."

Granger stretched past Pam's head to give his daughter a kiss on the cheek. "It's my life, my party, and my engagement. Deal with it."

"Oh, I'm dealing, all right. Can I see the ring?"

Pam tugged off her gloves. "Haven't you already?" That would be a surprise.

"Not on your finger, I haven't." She took Pam's hand and oohed her admiration. "Good job, Dad. I hope you like it, Pam."

"I really do. It's perfect. I'm not one for big, fancy jewelry."

"I knew that." Granger smirked.

She elbowed his gut. "Conceited much?"

All three laughed as they went inside. Pam looked around. Wow, they'd been busy since Pam had been here to decorate the tree with Granger yesterday afternoon. Both kids' school photos hung framed on the hallway wall, while a stunning painting of Jewel Lake hung above the fireplace. The mantel had been decorated with battery-operated tealights amid greenery and red bows.

She turned to Melissa. "This is gorgeous. It looks like a home."

"Aside from 20 folding chairs around the edge of the living room."

Pam laughed. "Aside from that. Look at the time! We'd better get ready for guests."

Granger saluted. "That's my cue. I'll grab your totes from the car. Back in a jiffy." He headed back out the door.

"Are you upset with him?" Pam needed to know.

"Nah, it's okay. I mean, we'd made plans, but I should have known he'd be more comfortable without an audience. I mean, what if you'd turned him down?"

"I never would have!"

Melissa laughed. "He knew that, but still. Anyway, now we have three reasons to party today. Dad's new home, his birthday, and your engagement. Welcome to the family, Pam."

"Thanks." Pam and Melissa were going to be the best of friends. She could see it already. "Where are the kids?"

"They'll walk over in a little while. It's only a few blocks, and they're both feeling up to it."

"Sidney's headaches?"

"Lessened, thankfully."

"I've been praying for her. For you."

"Thanks. We can talk about that later. I hear Dad at the door, so let's start laying out the food."

Pam rested her hands on the high-top table Granger had purchased for the breakfast nook. It added counter space to the small kitchen. Today, it would act as an island for the buffet. In a few months, it would be the spot where they ate their breakfast, lingered over coffee, and made plans for the day.

She blinked and shook her head. That was for the future. Today, they'd host the first of many parties in this cozy home.

Melissa set the first tote on the counter and turned to meet her dad at the door with the next.

Pam turned on the electric oven to heat the appetizers that required it. Granger was still looking for a gas range and a contractor to install it.

How had Granger made so many friends in Jewel Lake when he'd been a loner most of his life? God was so good. His little home bustled with a couple of dozen people, Pam's friends from Maranatha, Monte Newman, Vance and Loretta Satterfield, and a bunch of church friends, too, including the worship leader, Caleb, and his wife, Sage.

He nodded at Melissa.

She clinked a spoon against her glass. "Speech! Speech!"

The group quieted and turned to Granger just as Pam slipped her hand into his. He'd kiss her right now if everyone wasn't watching, though what did it matter? No, he'd wait a minute.

"Thanks, everyone, for coming. Today's a very special day, indeed, and I'm honored you all would come and share it with me. It's not every day a man turns 60."

A cheer went up.

Granger chuckled. "It's also not every day a man buys a house, though perhaps oftener than hitting a certain age marker."

Another cheer. It must be Laura inspiring those.

"But the most exciting thing about today is that, last night, I asked Pam to marry me, and she agreed." He lifted their joined hands together, making sure her ring was visible. "My life was forever changed by moving to Jewel Lake to get to know my daughter."

"You'd have turned 60 wherever you were," Audrey hollered.

Everyone laughed.

"True, that. But not with all of you to celebrate with me. I'm overwhelmed with gratitude to all of you, to Pam, and especially to my Lord and Savior, Jesus Christ. And so, with Christmas just a few days away, I'd like to take this moment to pray."

Heads ducked around the room. Pam's hand squeezed his.

"Father God, we come to You today, humbly grateful for all that You have done. We are thankful for the birth of Your Son, our Savior, Jesus. More than that, we are thankful for Jesus's death and resurrection that gives all of us new hope and a reason for living. All we can say is thank You. As Psalm 136:1 says, 'Give thanks to the Lord, for he is good, for his steadfast love endures forever.' So we are here, giving thanks. We trust You with the future. Thank You, Father. In the name of Your Son, amen."

Voices murmured, "Amen," from all around the room. "Thank You, Jesus."

Pam slid her arm around his waist, and he reciprocated as others turned to their own conversations. "Have I told you today that I love you?"

He tapped his jaw. "You may have mentioned something, but that was over an hour ago, and I'm not sure I remember it clearly."

"Do we need to have your memory tested already?" She raised her eyebrows.

Granger chuckled and kissed her lightly. "Okay, fine, I remember it, but I don't mind hearing it again."

"Silly man. I love you."

"I love you, too. Tell me, when can we make this official? I'm getting old. Sixty already! Don't wait until my mental faculties decline further to marry me."

"In a hurry, are we?"

"Yes?"

"I guess we'll need to talk about timing."

"We could elope tomorrow."

"We could, but we won't."

"Darn."

Melissa cleared her throat and looked between them. "I'd like to help plan your wedding, but if I do, don't you dare jump the gun and throw all the plans away last minute."

Granger laughed and pulled his daughter into their hug. "Promise."

Epilogue

Do. Not. Cry.

Not that Wendy Clarke could will herself to do anything. If she could, she'd start with being 120 pounds instead of... she had no idea of the actual number, nor did she wish to find out.

Thus, crying while Pam and Granger exchanged their wedding vows was a foregone conclusion. She dabbed at her eyes. Hopefully, she was being careful enough with the makeup her daughter Selah had applied with a delicate hand. Both Selah and Faith had returned to Jewel Lake for their Christmas vacation — Wendy refused to call it winter break, which cut the importance of Jesus's birth out of the equation — and been offered summer jobs by Julia.

Much to Wendy's surprise. Maybe she hadn't lost everything when Cheater Dave blew up her life. Not that she hadn't deserved his unfaithfulness. Look at her.

No, don't.

She was not going there. Not today, no matter how her childhood friend Audrey had blinked at Wendy's dress and turned away. Had Wendy expected a compliment? Not from Audrey. Not from anyone. Seventeen-year-old Faith did say the color looked good on her, so that was a win.

Look at Pam. She's glowing.

She should be. She's slim, and Granger adores her.

Pam's grief might have been very different from Wendy's, but no less real. And now, she'd met a fabulous man and was remarrying at the age of 54.

That would never be Wendy's fate. Marriage was for life, and Dave the Dud wasn't Dave the Dead. Just chasing after his second wife, who'd cheated on him. *How does rejection make you feel, Dave?* Not that she'd ever ask him.

Pam. Focus on Pam.

Trim, petite Pam in a cream, flowy, knee-length dress, a stunning bouquet of spring flowers, and a sparkling headpiece. Apparently veils had been out for a long time. Even Wendy's daughter Adriel hadn't worn one when she married Liam five years ago… merely weeks before her parents' marriage proved to be a farce.

Wendy had been planning their 25th wedding anniversary party when Dave told her not to bother, as they weren't going to make it that long.

Pam. Focus on Pam.

But she was sliding a thick platinum band on Granger's finger, made more difficult by the fact that she'd locked eyes with her groom, and neither of them were looking at their hands.

Laura sang a beautiful song about love, and Wendy managed not to scoff out loud. As if Laura knew anything about lasting love. Nor did Wendy. The only one of their group who'd had a happy marriage was Julia. Pam had finally admitted what they all suspected, that she and Mark had struggled, and they'd even separated for a time. They'd planned to try to work through their issues, and then the accident happened.

Why couldn't it have been Dave the Adulterer who'd been hit by a semi-truck?

Uncharitable, Wendy.

Yeah, yeah. That would have been too handy.

"May I present to you Mr. and Mrs. Granger Durand?"

The Creekside Fellowship auditorium erupted into cheers as Pam and Granger shared another kiss before practically dancing their way to the foyer.

"Well, that was a nice wedding, as they go." Audrey's voice came from the pew behind Wendy.

Wendy turned. Was Audrey speaking to her? Apparently. She forced a smile and hoped, once again, that she hadn't smeared her mascara. "Yes. Lovely."

"I'm never marrying again."

Something she and Audrey agreed on. Pretty rare since Bible school days.

"Did I tell you Roman's coming later this summer? I haven't seen him in ages."

"You did mention that." Wendy's girls joined the rest of the people lining up to leave the sanctuary. "I haven't seen him since your wedding. Even then, I could hardly believe he was a teenager! I wouldn't have recognized him."

Audrey shook her head. "Teen no longer. He's in his forties."

"Married?" Not that it mattered.

"No. I think Steve and I cured him of any desire that our parents may have left. We never made marriage look attractive."

Wendy had thought she and Dave did. Hadn't it been perfect? He'd supported her desire to be a stay-at-home, homeschooling mom. He'd eagerly participated in the creation of their six children. He'd provided for every need.

Until, one day, he proved it had all been a farce.

Her bubble of perfection had turned out to be a balloon that a single pinprick could pop. And while it seemed some couples could regroup from a broken marriage — like Sheryl and Ted Johannesson — most could not. Wendy'd hoped and prayed that Dave would see the light and return, penitent. She would graciously accept his fervent apology, and they'd be happier than ever.

But Dave the Dumb chased after his 30-year-old second wife who'd cheated on him. Just like Wendy had chased after him.

It was not a good look.

"Roman asked about you."

Wendy blinked as she looked back at Audrey. The church was all but empty now. "He did? I'm surprised he remembers me."

"I mentioned that all my college friends had regathered here. He said, 'Wendy, too? She's single again?'" Audrey rolled her eyes. "I don't know why he wondered."

Wendy had no clue. He'd been a toddler when she and Audrey had first been friends, tagging along behind them. Both their parents had worked, and babysitting had been Audrey's job. Wendy hadn't minded, for the most part. He was a cute kid, and much too young to care about the secrets she and Audrey had whispered to each other.

They didn't share secrets anymore. Audrey spent too much time slamming Wendy's body shape for that.

Wendy pulled to her feet. "I guess we should take our turn to congratulate the bride and groom."

Audrey rose smoothly, elegantly, not like a hippo coming out of the water. "You and Melissa planned the reception, right?"

"Yes. Mostly Melissa."

"You've done a good job with events at the inn."

Wendy blinked. Had Audrey actually complimented her? Was that still a thing?

"You don't need to look so shocked. I can be honest."

As if that had ever been in doubt. "Thank you."

"You're welcome." Audrey poked her chin toward the back. "Come on. Let's go."

Had a new era of friendship just begun? If so, Wendy would take it.

A Note...

Dear Wendy,

You've got a long row to hoe, my dear friend, and it may surprise you to learn that Audrey's "little" brother will play a major role in it! Stick with me, Wendy. Stick with Jesus, who will give you a new view of yourself. A new hope, if you will.

Your loving author,

Valerie

Dear Reader,

I hope you loved Pam and Granger's story! It's been a refreshing change to write older characters with their unique challenges in life.

Wendy and Roman's story is next in *Her Hopeful Heart*. Do I think every homeschooling mom has six kids, is overweight, and suffers from low self-esteem? OF COURSE NOT! This is simply the way Wendy entered my mind and the Maranatha Inn series! I hope you'll give her a chance. I've come to love Wendy intensely, and I hope you will, too.

Blessings, Valerie

https://valeriecomer.com/hopeful

Acknowledgments

Thank you, dear readers, for your words of praise for the free novella, *Her Waiting Heart,* and your enthusiasm to see *Her Thankful Heart* come to fruition! It's a departure from my usual cowboy and farm-fresh romances, but I've been enjoying it. I'm glad you have, too.

Thanks to my writing buddies who check in with me often with encouragement and a kick in the rear as needed. Jan Thompson, Lynnette Bonner, and Elizabeth Maddrey — this writing gig would be so lonely without you! And I'm happy to return the favor. ;)

Thanks, Nicole, for editing so very many of my stories by now! I appreciate your wit, your guidance, and your faithfulness. I hope I never have to find a new editor!

Thanks to my family for believing in me and giving me the time and space to work. To my husband, Jim, for his steadfast care and encouragement. To my kids and grandkids, thanks for your understanding, too!

But most of all, thanks to Jesus, the Author and Finisher of my faith. I write for Your glory, Jesus. Thank you for everything. Literally… everything.

Dear Reader...

Thanks for reading *Her Thankful Heart*! I'm so honored that you chose to spend the last few hours with Pam, Granger, and me. You are appreciated.

I'm an independent author who relies on my readers to help spread the word about stories you enjoy. Would you take a few minutes to let your friends know? Facebook, Instagram, Goodreads... wherever you hang out online.

Also, each honest review at online retailers means a lot to me and helps other readers know if this is a book they might enjoy. I'd sure appreciate your help getting word out!

I welcome contact from readers. At my website, you can contact me via email, read my blog, and find me on social media. You can also sign up for my newsletter to be notified of new releases, contests, special deals, and more! You'll receive *Her Waiting Heart*, the novella that introduces the Christmas at Maranatha Inn series, absolutely free as my thank you gift!

~ Valerie Comer

www.valeriecomer.com

https://valeriecomer.com/waiting

Books by Valerie Comer

You'll find the complete list of titles by Valerie Comer on her website: fifty books (and counting) in ten series (and counting)! Come on over to find farm-fresh romance, cowboy romance, and small-town romance, all with distinctly Christian themes.

https://valeriecomer.com/books

About Valerie Comer

Valerie Comer is constantly amazed that living, talking, dreaming characters appear in her mind and flow from her fingertips and, from there, to her delighted readers. She only hopes her creations enjoy their happily-ever-afters as much as she does hers, sharing rural life in western Canada with her husband, adult children, and adorable grandkids.

Valerie is a two-time *USA Today* bestselling author and a two-time Word Award winner. She is known for writing engaging characters, strong communities, and deep faith into her green clean romances.

To find out more, visit her website at www.valeriecomer.com, where you can read her blog, explore her many links, and sign up for her email newsletter, where you will find news, giveaways, deals, book recommendations and more.